THE THIRD EYE

EI-80

THE THIRD EYE

Mahtab Narsimhan

THE DUNDURN GROUP
TORONTO

Editor: Barry Jowett   Design: Alison Carr
Printer: Webcom

Library and Archives Canada Cataloguing in Publication

Narsimhan, Mahtab

    The third eye / Mahtab Narsimhan.

ISBN 978-1-55002-750-1

    I. Title.

PS8627.A77T45 2007   jC813'.6   C2007-905459-5

1   2   3   4   5   11   10   09   08   07

Canada   Conseil des Arts du Canada   Canada Council for the Arts   ONTARIO ARTS COUNCIL CONSEIL DES ARTS DE L'ONTARIO

We acknowledge the support of **The Canada Council for the Arts** and the **Ontario Arts Council** for our publishing program. We also acknowledge the financial support of the Government of Canada through the Book Publishing Industry Development Program and **The Association for the Export of Canadian Books**, and the Government of Ontario through the **Ontario Book Publishers Tax Credit** program, and the **Ontario Media Development Corporation**.

Care has been taken to trace the ownership of copyright material used in this book. The author and the publisher welcome any information enabling them to rectify any references or credits in subsequent editions.

J. Kirk Howard, President

Printed and bound in Canada.
Printed on recycled paper.
www.dundurn.com

Dundurn Press
3 Church Street, Suite 500
Toronto, Ontario, Canada
M5E 1M2

Gazelle Book Services Limited
White Cross Mills
High Town, Lancaster, England
LA1 4XS

Dundurn Press
2250 Military Road
Tonawanda, NY
U.S.A. 14150

For Dad, who inspired this story.
For Mom, who kept me going.
And for Rahul, Aftab, and Coby,
the three favourite men in my life.

PROLOGUE

Someone was following him. He was sure of it. Bare feet following in time to his steps and stopping just after he did. Late enough to be heard, soon enough not to give away their direction.

Shakti hesitated. He looked around. The deepening gloom in the forest cast eerie shadows across the path. A biting wind swept down from the Shivalik Range and woke every tree and shrub in its path. Shakti shivered, more from fear than cold. He cursed himself for losing track of the time and wandering so far away from the safety of his village, Morni.

Holding up the lantern, he peered intently for any sign of his pursuers. Darkness surged against the edges of the feeble light. He lowered the lantern and hurried toward the village.

His sturdy leather mojris ground up the dead leaves.

Bare feet followed.

He quickened his pace.

The pursuers matched it.

His heart thumped like a tom-tom within his chest. He dropped the dead hares slung over his shoulder and bolted, his lantern knocking against his knee. The flame flickered and went out. He was plunged into darkness. The sickly sweet smell of rotting flesh wafted past him. Panicked, he went crashing through the trees, not caring about the noise he made. He had to get to the village before they caught him. The footsteps were louder now, coming closer and closer. His breath came in gasps as he ran. He tripped and fell headlong into the bushes. Dirt filled his mouth. It tasted like wet earth mixed with worms. He spat it out. Sharp rocks scraped his chest in spite of his thick kurta. He put his hands on the ground to push himself up when a heavy body landed on his back. One, two, three ... he lost count of how many bodies piled on top of him, holding him down. It felt like huge boulders had landed on his back and knocked the air out of his lungs. He smelled their breaths — which reeked like a combination of rotten eggs and feces — and almost vomited.

"Please," he gibbered. "Please don't hurt me."

A warning thump on the head silenced him. The weight on his back began to lighten till the only thing pinning him on the ground was the rough skin of a foot planted in the small of his back. He tried to twist his head back to see who it was, but the complete darkness made identification impossible. He waited, sweat dripping into his eyes, bile nestled at the base of his throat just waiting to erupt.

Suddenly, the gloom dissipated. Someone was coming toward him bearing a lit torch. He looked up at his captors and his stomach contracted with fear. A sea of ghastly green faces looked down at him. A huge, green monstrosity towered over Shakti. The monster's skin was stretched tight over his gaunt, skull-like face and framed by dirt-encrusted hair. Eyes, black as bottomless pools, bored into Shakti. Then he noticed the man's chest. The skin was translucent and he could see all the way to the man's heart — a pulsing fist pumping black liquid through that massive body. It was fascinating, yet horrifying, to watch the green body criss-crossed with a network of black.

Shakti's eyes strayed upward again to the man's face. A deep gash ran the length of his forehead. It was still fresh, and black liquid seeped from the edges of the swollen skin. The man, clearly the leader of the group, stared at him with his whiteless eyes. Shakti looked around at the sea of bodies, which looked the same except that the shape and size of that horrifying form varied. They all had similar gashes on their foreheads, though some of the wounds seemed to have healed while others looked very fresh.

They pressed closer to Shakti, touching, pinching, and prodding him with grimy fingers. He stood up on shaky legs, desperately looking for an opening in the crowd. The sickly smell enveloped him and seemed to permeate his body through every pore.

"What do you want?" he croaked.

Silence.

The giant who blocked his path raised a callused green hand with filthy, black fingernails up to Shakti's eye level. Shakti jumped backward, lost his balance, and fell to the ground. He turned to crawl away, sobbing with terror, but was barred by a fence of feet — feet that looked unnatural because they were all *turned backwards at the ankle*! A scream rose in his throat. He jumped up, arms outstretched, pushing his way through the crowd. Someone grabbed him by the hair and jerked his head back. He felt a razor-sharp fingernail move across his forehead, tearing through the tender skin. A searing pain coursed from his head through his body like liquid fire. The pain was so intense that he was starting to lose consciousness. Through the haze he saw a tall figure approaching.

Maniacal laughter echoed around him and then everything went dark.

CHAPTER 1
THE BLACK COBRA

A bright burst of stars lit the night sky, illuminating the upturned faces of the children gathered around the old banyan tree. The stars dissolved into smoke and it was dark again. Laughter rang out from the clearing where a dozen children of the village of Morni had gathered for the festival of lights. The smoke and smell of gunpowder hung in the air.

A short distance away from the clearing, two silent forms sat huddled on the front step of their hut. Tara hugged her younger brother, Suraj, as they watched the firework display. Around them, Morni shimmered in the glow of clay lamps that adorned homes and doorways as far as Tara could see. The soft, yellow light reflected off the reds, greens, and blues of the villagers' clothes and their gold and silver jewellery. They were all dressed in their best to celebrate the joyous occasion of Diwali, the New Year of the Hindus.

She heard a deep sigh.

"Cheer up, Suraj," said Tara. "Mother will be back next year." She had doubts that this was true, but for the sake of her brother she had to keep up a brave front. She looked up at the black sky, now strewn with stars, and for the umpteenth time she whispered a plea.

"I'm so scared, Lord Ganesh, so scared. But please don't let anyone find out ... especially Suraj. And send Mother back to us."

A solitary tear rolled down her cheek and she wiped it away as she glanced at her brother. He was so thin and small; he did not look seven years old, more like five. His skin was a deep brown from working in the hot sun. Unruly black hair surrounded a pinched face and black eyes that had once sparkled with mischief, now long gone. His white kurta pyjama hung on his bony frame.

They sat in silence looking up at the stars. Suraj rested his head in Tara's lap.

"Why won't anyone play with us anymore, Didi?" asked Suraj with a wobble in his voice. "Didi" was the respectful way to address an older sister.

"I don't know, Suraj," said Tara, staring into the distance.

"Where is Mother, Didi? Why did she go away? Why?" asked Suraj, his voice barely above a whisper.

Tara tightened her grip on his shoulders. She had no answers to his anguished questions. Her mind turned back to a morning almost a year ago, a few days after Diwali, when her mother had woken her while it was still very dark outside. Rubbing the sleep out of her eyes, she had noticed that her mother was dressed to go out. She had looked very upset and sad as she hugged Tara close to her.

"I have to go away, my child."

Tara's heart beat at triple speed. She pushed her mother's arms away and stared at her in complete shock.

"Go away? Where? I'm coming with you."

"No, Tara. You have to look after your brother. But I will be back. I promise we will all be together again."

Tara clung to her mother's skirt, sobbing softly, feeling as if she were in a bad dream. Her mother undid a gold chain from her neck and fastened it around Tara's neck. On it hung a small, bejewelled mirror shaped like an equilateral triangle. The border was inlaid with red stones in hues of the setting sun. These were interspersed with blue star-shaped stones, the shade of a summer sky. Leaves in thin, gold filigree wound their way around the border. Of the little jewellery her mother owned, this was Tara's favourite.

"Wear this always, Tara, and when you look into it, you will find strength."

"Mother, don't leave me, please," said Tara, sobbing even harder.

Her father, Shiv, and Suraj were still fast asleep.

"Hush, my child. We will be together again, I promise."

"Parvati, it's time. We have to go," someone called out very softly from the window.

Parvati looked up and nodded. She took Tara's face in her hands and looked deep into her eyes.

"I have to go, Tara. Be brave, be strong, and remember: always do the right thing."

She kissed Tara's forehead and Tara was suddenly overcome with sleep. As she fought to keep her eyes open, she glimpsed her mother dousing the lantern and then she was gone.

● ● ●

Tara blinked. A purple cone was spewing silver and gold stars into the night sky.

"Didi, do you think our friends will mind if I join them?"

Tara was silent for a moment, then said,

"But you have no crackers to share with them."

"So what?" asked Suraj in a belligerent tone.

Tara took a deep breath. "Next year. Let's just enjoy watching them, okay?"

"Okay," said Suraj as he snuggled closer.

Tara heard snatches of conversation:

"Mala, taste the kheer I made ..."

"Oh, what a beautiful yellow outfit. Who stitched it for you?"

"Children, we're starting prayers for the goddess Lakshmi. Bring your father and come inside immediately."

Tara and Suraj sat quietly, listening to the happy voices

around them, when the loud beating of a drum overpowered the sound of the crackers that reverberated from every corner of the village. A swarthy man in an orange robe appeared near the banyan tree, a large drum hanging from a rope circling his neck.

"Hear, hear ... Come one, come all," he called out in a sing-song voice. "I have exciting news."

His sudden appearance caught everyone's attention. They gathered in the clearing, looking expectantly at the drummer. Tara and Suraj stood up to get a better look. The dark-skinned man looked at the silent faces and once again sang.

"On this auspicious day of Diwali, I present to you the greatest healer of all. He has decided to grace this village with his presence. The one and only ZAAAAAARRRRKKKUUUUUU."

He yelled the last word slowly as a man in a black, flowing robe stepped out from the shadows of the banyan tree and into the light. The crowd gasped as one and fell silent. He was tall with broad shoulders. There was not a single hair on his head and the lamplight flickering off his bald pate gave it a golden sheen. He had a long, thin nose and a prominent jaw. But it was his eyes that instantly drew everyone's attention. They were black, tar black. There seemed to be no whites at all and this made him look oddly menacing in spite of the benevolent smile on his face.

It seemed to Tara as if she were looking into a deep, bottomless well. She shivered involuntarily and noticed that a lot of people were shifting uneasily, whispering to each other and pointing at the newcomer's pulsing forehead. In the dim light and from a distance, Tara could not make out what it was, but it looked like ... Could it be? ... Was it possible? ... A *third eye*?

A brash young villager stepped forward and voiced the question that, Tara had no doubt, was in every villager's mind.

"What is that on your forehead?" he asked rudely.

Zarku's eyes narrowed.

"You mean this?" said Zarku, touching the bulge on his forehead lightly.

The man nodded.

"This is the Eye of Truth. It looks beyond the body into the heart and mind. I can sense strength and weakness in people, I can see illness before it blossoms, I can see a crime before it is committed. And I can see what is in your mind at the moment," he said, snickering.

The young man looked bewildered.

"Want me to tell a certain young woman to meet you near the Ganesh temple at midnight?"

The boy blanched and shook his head frantically as his eyes darted to a pretty young girl in a yellow kurta pyjama who had pulled a dupatta over her face.

The young man shuffled backward and melted into the crowd.

"People of Morni," said Zarku in a cold, penetrating voice, lifting his hairless, white arms to the heavens, "I have come in answer to your prayers. I know that you have lost your own healer recently. I come on Diwali, the first day of our New Year, to heal pain and alleviate any suffering. There will never be sickness in the village. Health and prosperity shall be the future of Morni and every village for miles around."

Murmurs peppered the air.

"Who are you?" asked the village chief, Raka, stepping forward. Raka was a wiry man with a wrinkled face and gnarled hands. His innocuous look belied the wisdom that lay behind the shrewd, brown eyes. He ruled the village of Morni with a firm and just hand, with the help of four elders that formed the Panchayat.

"I am Zarku, the best healer in all of India. I am compelled to go where I am most needed."

"We did not ask you to come, thank you very much," snapped a village elder.

"Patience, my good men," said Dushta, the village moneylender. "We do need a healer. Zarku, show us your powers. Why should we believe you are the greatest healer?"

A slow smile spread over Zarku's face. The bulge on his forehead twitched and flickered. A deep furrow appeared just above his eyes. His smile chilled Tara till goose bumps rose on her arms. She moved closer to Suraj as he clutched her arm.

"He does not look very nice, Didi," whispered Suraj. "There is something about him that is ..."

"Evil," said Tara, looking at Suraj's scared expression. She put an arm around his shoulders.

Zarku beckoned to a villager, Lalu, standing nearby. Lalu looked aghast at being singled out. He stood there for a moment, eyes darting. When Raka nodded, he shuffled forward. Zarku closed his eyes and the one on his forehead popped open. The crowd gasped. Silver light bathed Lalu from head to toe. Lalu stood quietly without moving a muscle.

"You suffer from chest infections and an extra-hairy back, which your wife hates. And there is a cure if you want to see me later."

People tittered in the background.

"Yes," said Lalu, glaring at the crowd, "you're right, Zarku, there is no need to go on."

"Is there anyone here who does not believe in my powers? This is but child's play. Death and illness dare not linger where I am," he said, his voice thundering over the crowd.

"Impressive, Zarku. But the hour is late. The Panchayat will meet in the morning to decide if Morni needs you," said Raka. "Tonight is Diwali, and we are all about to start the Lakshmi pooja — prayers for the Goddess of Wealth. I welcome you to spend the night in the guest hut. Dinner will be served to you shortly."

He joined his hands in a namaste and turned to go, a puzzled expression still lingering on his face.

"No need for the guest hut," said Dushta. "Zarku can

stay with me."

Raka nodded, and Dushta led Zarku to his hut while the crowd dispersed. Tara and Suraj sat down. The excitement over, they waited for their father, Shiv, and stepmother, Kali, to return home from visiting the neighbours and prepare dinner. Delicious smells wafted out from the neighbouring huts, making their stomachs growl with hunger.

"Didi, I'm so hungry, is there anything to eat?" asked Suraj.

She looked at his starved face, stood up, and walked into the hut to rummage through the kitchen. She knew exactly where to look and hoped the cache was still there. Fear and hunger jostled inside her. Kali always kept some sweets in a glass jar on the topmost shelf in case her darling, overfed daughter, Layla, wanted a snack before a huge meal.

Tara climbed onto the bottom shelf of the kitchen, stepped to the one above, and reached out for the jar on the top shelf. She inched it forward with her fingertips, her hands slippery with sweat. She knew they were already in trouble. But today was Diwali and tradition was to celebrate the start of the New Year with something sweet.

As soon as her slippery fingers grasped the jar, she jumped down and opened it eagerly to examine the contents. Two small laddoos, sweets made of lentils and sugar, lay at the bottom. *Put it back, put it back*, said the small voice inside her. But the hunger was too strong. She ran out to Suraj, ignoring the voice.

"Here you are, Suraj, Happy Diwali!" she said as she handed him one laddoo and took the other. They ate the laddoos and watched the fireworks, which had started up again. The laddoo tasted bitter to her and Tara regretted having stolen them. Suraj had already finished his so she handed him the rest of hers.

"Are you sure, Didi?" he asked.

"I'm sure," she said.

She put the empty jar beside her and gazed into the distance.

Suraj snuggled up to Tara and she put her arm around him. She thought of this time last year, when they had also been part of the festivities. If she had only known of the sorrow awaiting them in the New Year, she would have cherished every minute spent with her mother instead of taking her presence for granted.

Tara was jerked out of her reverie by two unpleasant incidents: an exploding firecracker, and a particularly hard slap on her face.

"Wha...?" said Tara as she shot to her feet, holding her hand to her stinging cheek.

Suraj had fallen asleep with his head in Tara's lap. He jumped up, too, his eyes wide with terror. Their stepmother, Kali, towered over them. Anger and hate twisted her face into an ugly mask. The little black eyes in her fat face looked like small raisins in an unusually large, uncooked, ball of dough.

"How *dare* you touch any food in the house without my

permission?" she yelled, eyeing the empty jar beside them. "I told you I would be back to give you a meal, didn't I?"

Tara's heart sank. *I told you not to steal the laddoos*, said the small voice inside her.

"I'm sorry, Mother," she said in a soft, pleading tone, hating herself for not standing up to Kali.

She looked up in mute appeal at her father, standing silently behind Kali, who was still berating them. Red spittle from the paan Kali was chewing flecked Tara's face. Her father brushed past her and entered the hut without saying a word.

"Go to bed, both of you. NOW!" said Kali. "You have been very bad children, stealing your poor sister's sweets."

As if on cue their stepsister, Layla, peeked out from behind her mother's ample body, stuck out her tongue at them, and ran inside.

"But I'm so hungry," said Suraj, tears filling his eyes.

"You should have thought of that before stealing in your own home," snapped Kali.

Tara knew she was responsible for this. If she had amused Suraj somehow till Kali came back ...

She cringed inside as the tears cascaded down Suraj's cheeks. Gently, she steered him into the hut and made for a corner of their two-room mud hut to make their bed for the night. She unrolled a thin, straw mat on the floor and curled up on it with Suraj. Shaking out a torn, threadbare sheet, she covered them both and closed her eyes to block out Kali's malevolent stare, which followed their every move. Finally, her stepmother moved away into the kitchen to prepare the evening meal and Tara could breathe peacefully.

The fragrance of freshly boiled basmati rice and chicken curry wafted to where they lay. Tara's stomach grumbled in protest. She heard an answering grumble from her brother's stomach. They both loved chicken curry.

"I hate you, Kali," she whispered under her breath, feeling weak, hungry, and very tired.

Her fingers sought the gold chain around her neck. She slid her hand along the chain and pulled out the mirror her mother had given her. She always kept it hidden from Kali lest that cruel woman take away this last memento of Parvati's, which Tara treasured more than any other possession. She held it up and, by the light of the lantern, looked into the mirror. The red stones seemed to be on fire and the blue stones swirled with shadows.

Soft brown eyes in a thin face with high cheekbones stared back at her. There were deep shadows under her eyes. The full mouth, normally upturned at the corners, seemed to be drooping. Thick brown shoulder-length hair, well oiled and plaited, framed her face. The only sparkle in her face was from a tiny silver nose stud that she wore.

"Where are you, Mother? We miss you so much," she whispered.

Suraj moved closer to Tara.

"Why did Mother go away, Didi? WHY? I *hate* her for leaving us!"

"Shh, Suraj, I am sure she had a reason, though I wish I knew what it was."

Almost a year had gone by and they had not seen their mother or their grandfather, who had both disappeared on the same day. The worst part was that no one wanted to talk about it or answer any questions. It was maddening! There were a hundred questions in her mind and no answers. *Why had they disappeared? Where were they now? Were they dead? And the most important, would they ever come back?*

Tara held on to the belief that her mother would be back, like a drowning person hanging on to a floating piece of wood. If she let go of that belief, she would drown in the sorrow that seemed to be swirling around her. What would happen to Suraj then?

At long last the sounds of smacking and slurping subsided. Both she and Suraj pretended to be asleep as soon as they heard Kali come into the room to make up her bed. Kali and Layla shared a cot and Shiv had another one. Tara and Suraj slept on the floor because there were no more spare cots. Soon, everyone was in bed and the lantern was doused.

Moonlight filtered in through the window in the front room, making bright patterns on the mud floor. Tara shivered as a frigid gust of wind ruffled through the straw on the roof and swept in through the cracks. A cloud moved across the face of the moon and plunged the room into momentary darkness. Tara moved closer to Suraj, the warmth of his body comforting her. She was thankful for the thick, woollen clothes, which afforded some padding on the cold, hard floor. She could not sleep. In the distance, she heard a stray dog barking. The incessant sounds of lizards, as they ran around the outer wall of the hut seeking flies, kept her company. The cloud passed and moonlight lay in silver puddles on the floor once again.

Suraj whimpered in his sleep and turned restlessly.

"Mother," he whispered.

Tara stroked his forehead, shushing him. Her heart ached to see that even in his sleep, Suraj was troubled. She stroked his hair tenderly and Suraj stopped his restless tossing and turning.

At long last, she started to feel drowsy. As her eyelids drooped, she saw a slight movement on the mud-packed floor a few feet from where she lay. Her eyes widened and her sleep vanished in an instant, blood turning to ice as she sat bolt upright. A black cobra, the deadliest snake in India, uncoiled its length and raised its hood, ready to strike. In the bright moonlight, cobra and girl stared at each other in absolute silence, not a movement to betray that either was breathing. Suddenly, the cobra lowered is hood and, with lightning speed, covered the last few feet between itself and the sleeping form of Suraj. It stopped next to Suraj and once again raised its hood, swaying menacingly from side to side.

CHAPTER 2
THE PEACOCK'S TAIL

Tara froze.

She could not scream or move, so great was her fear born of thousands of tales she had heard about the fatality of a cobra's bite. The snake slithered over the sleeping form of Suraj, closer and closer to his forehead. It stopped and raised its hood, preparing to strike. Silver light glinted off the spectacle-like markings on its hood.

Tara lunged sideways, grabbed her leather shoe, and raised her hand to hurl it at the cobra. All of a sudden the snake faced her. Coiled on Suraj's sleeping form, its eyes were almost level with Tara's. Her hand stopped in mid-air and, inexplicably, her fear melted away. She was looking into black eyes that seemed gentle, almost sad.

The cobra swayed toward her right hand. Its forked tongue flicked out and caressed Tara's bare forearm. An image of her family, when they were all together, flashed through her mind like a bolt of lightning, filling her with joy. In an instant, the image faded away. Speechless, she watched as the cobra then flicked its blood-red tongue on Suraj's forehead so lightly and gently that the boy's sleep was undisturbed.

The spot where the cobra's tongue touched Tara's skin felt warm. She ran her fingertips over the flesh. There was nothing, not even a puncture. No tingling feeling to indicate that a deadly poison was coursing through her veins.

The cobra took a last look at Tara. With a fluid, silvery movement, it slithered off Suraj's body, raced across the mud floor, and disappeared into a hole in the far corner of the hut. Tara stooped over Suraj anxiously. His chest rose and fell as he continued his deep sleep. Tara lay back on the straw mat, drawing in great gulps of air to slow her racing heart.

What had just happened? The deadliest of snakes in India had touched them with its forked tongue and they were both alive to tell the tale. Who would believe her if she said anything about this? No one to her knowledge had ever survived an encounter with a cobra.

She fell asleep after a very long time.

• • •

The day after Diwali dawned cold and grey. A glacial wind crept through the cracks, poking and prodding people with its cold fingers.

Tara awoke as an icy draught swept over her exposed face. Light was seeping in through the corners of the window. Tara tiptoed to it, eager to see the sunrise. As she peered out the window, she noticed that Raka, whose hut was diagonally opposite theirs, was awake, too. He sat on a wooden chair on the porch sipping a cup of tea. Steam curled up from the cooling tea, obscuring his face. In front of them stood the banyan tree, trunk firmly planted in the earth, branches outstretched to welcome the day. The long roots swayed lazily in the wind. Everyone slept and the silence was broken only by the wind sighing through the leaves. They both saw it at the same time: a brilliant flash of colour near the tree. A peacock, with a beautiful tail of gold and blue, cavorted into the open.

Tara shot to her feet and watched, mesmerized, as the peacock spread its tail so that it fanned out behind its emerald blue body. The bird danced in the clearing as the sky turned grey and shards of lightning illuminated the dazzling blue, green, and gold in its plumage. Raka jumped to his feet, too. The teacup crashed to the ground, brown liquid staining the bottom of his white pyjamas. The peacock's dancing grew more frenzied. Fat drops of rain pelted to the earth as the skies burst open. Some of the drops fell on the peacock and the "eyes" on its tail seemed to be crying. The peacock continued to pirouette in the clearing — solely, it seemed, for the benefit of Raka.

Suddenly, it came right up to where he stood and looked him directly in the eye. Its feathers spread in a vibrating fan of energy. It gave a long, harsh cry that seemed to reverberate through the empty clearing to the hills beyond. Then it turned and danced out of sight. Raka clenched his hands and stared into space. *Why does he look so shocked and scared?* Tara wondered. Surely a peacock was a thing of beauty that should be admired, not feared.

Tara was starting to feel drowsy again. Shutting the window, she tiptoed back to Suraj and lay down next to him, falling asleep almost instantly.

• • •

Someone yanked the thin sheet from Tara's body. The cold November-morning air flooded over her skin and she was instantly awake. Kali's disagreeable face looked down on her.

"Get up, you lazy girl. Feed the cow and chickens and then make me a cup of tea. Tell Suraj to get water from the well."

Before walking away, Kali prodded the sleeping Suraj hard with her toe. He woke up whimpering with pain and instinctively raised his hands to ward off a blow.

What a miserable start to the day, thought Tara as she saw his distress and fear. Tears misted her eyes as she got up, reluctant to let her stepmother see how upset she was. *Do something*, the little voice inside her said, but Tara did nothing. Kali's wrath would be worse if she or Suraj put up even the tiniest bit of resistance. Suddenly, the image of the night visit from the black cobra flashed into her mind and she felt a powerful jolt of happiness once again. She hugged Suraj, whispering in his ear that she had a wonderful secret to tell him. He looked up at her with an endearing eagerness at the word "secret" and said,

"Didi, I'll be good. Please tell me, tell me now ... what is this secret?"

Tara smiled.

"Not now, Suraj. The wicked witch will hear."

Both children smiled mischievously at this small form of rebellion.

Tara tidied up the front room while Suraj skipped into the kitchen and out through the back door to brush his teeth in the washing area in the courtyard. Within seconds he was back. He eyed the leftovers from last night and his stomach growled loudly. Tara walked up to him and hugged his thin frame.

"Give me some food, Didi, please."

"I can't, Suraj," said Tara in a pained voice. "You have to get the water first or that wicked witch will have another excuse to starve us."

Suraj's shoulders slumped and a sad expression clouded his face.

"Why can't Layla go? It's so unfair!"

Tara kneeled and took his hands in hers.

"Because I am asking *you*."

Suraj nodded, still looking sullen. His expression was a mixture of anger and deep sadness. He eyed the stale chappatis once again and then, without a word, picked up the empty earthen pot and walked out the back door.

"Come back soon and I'll have fresh chappatis and sweet tea ready for you," said Tara as they walked out to the backyard. She scattered grain to the five chickens and rooster as she watched Suraj shuffle out the gate. Tears sprang to her eyes and she bit her lip hard to stem the flow, determined not to give in *this* early in the day.

Tara then tended to their cow, Bela. Her mother, Parvati, had brought the cow as part of her dowry when she had wedded their father, Shiv. Bela was chocolate brown with white spots, soft brown eyes, and a large, wet nose. Bela gave less milk these days, but it was still enough for them. It seemed she, too, was pining away for Parvati.

As Tara milked Bela, she told her about the cobra visiting her in the night. Warm milk streamed through her fingers and into the bucket as she expertly pulled on the cow's teats. Bela stood quietly, swishing her tail to drive away the inevitable flies that settled on her back. As Tara reached the part when the snake had caressed her forearm with its forked tongue, Bela licked Tara on the cheek. Tara almost fell off the stool. She raised an eyebrow in surprise, but Bela was lazily chewing the cud as if nothing had happened.

"Bela, I wish you could talk," said Tara, standing up and stroking Bela on her broad, brown back.

"TARA, you miserable girl, where's my tea?" bellowed Kali.

Tara gave a start and, grabbing the bucket of milk, ran out of Bela's shed. She raced into the kitchen as fast as her slim legs would allow.

"What took you so long?" Kali demanded.

"Sorry, Mother," said Tara, almost choking on the second word. There was not the remotest resemblance between her mother and this evil witch. "Bela's stall was a bit messier than usual. I cleaned it as thoroughly as I could," she lied.

"I want my tea in the next five minutes or else. And then make some chappatis for your father before he leaves for the fields. I have a bad headache and I am going to lie down for a while. And yes, feed my Layla, too. Mind you don't skimp on the ghee. She's growing and needs a lot of nourishment."

"Yes, Mother," said Tara obediently, her eyes lowered, a storm of emotions raging inside her. Suraj and she were growing too, yet Kali starved them at every opportunity and took great pleasure in it.

Kali turned and walked away to the front of the hut and lay down on her cot with an audible sigh. Tara sat fuming, her hands clenched, wishing she had the strength to fight back. *You're a coward*, said the voice inside her. *I know*, she sighed.

Tara poked the ashes in the three-sided, raised, earthen platform that served as their stove. She struck a match to light the thin twigs and as they caught fire, she blew on them, adding a few dung cakes. Soon, a strong fire crackled, spreading a warm, earthy smell throughout the hut. Tara put a shiny steel vessel on top of the platform to boil water for tea. She kneaded cream-coloured wheat flour with salt and water to make dough. While she prepared tea, her father entered the kitchen and sat cross-legged in front of her. His eyes had a vacant look.

"How are you today, Tara?" he asked.

"I am fine, Father," she said, pouring tea into four glasses lined up in front of her. "I'll give Mother her tea and be back to make your chappatis."

She walked to the front room with the tea and put it by her mother's cot.

"Would you like something to eat?"

"Go away and don't disturb me," snapped Kali.

Tara was only too happy to get away from her. She went back to the kitchen, put a flat skillet on the fire, and drizzled a spoonful of ghee. The clarified butter spluttered and sizzled, sending out a mouth-watering aroma that made Tara's stomach ache with hunger. She rolled out the dough into a perfect round on a floured wooden board with a long, wooden rolling pin. She flipped the uncooked chappati onto the palm of her right hand and in one fluid movement transferred it to the skillet.

As the first chappati puffed up, a huge golden ball filled with steam, she had to use all her willpower to stop from grabbing and stuffing it into her mouth. She took a huge gulp of the tea to quell her hunger pangs and immediately blinked in pain as the hot tea scorched a trail down her throat. Her heat-hardened hands did not need tongs to flip the chappati. When it was ready, she deftly pinched its edge and transferred the golden-brown sphere to her father's steel plate, where he had already put a dab of pickles and an onion. It subsided into a flat round as the steam escaped. She started making the second one just as Suraj walked in, balancing the earthen pot on his head. He looked tired, and the day had just begun. He put the earthen pot by the door and bounded to her side.

"Make me one too, Didi. I am so hungry," he said, smacking his lips.

"Sit down," she said.

She placed a glass of tea in front of him and wordlessly looked at her father, asking permission to serve Suraj the next chappati. Her father nodded.

He looked so cold and aloof. She yearned for the love that she used to see in his eyes when their mother had been around. Had he forgotten that they were his children? Did he not love them anymore?

Where have you gone, Father? Who is this stranger in front of me? I don't know you at all, thought Tara as she continued making chappatis and dropping them into her father's and Suraj's plates alternately.

"I am HUNGRY. Give me some food," demanded Layla, flouncing into the room, her fat cheeks jiggling.

She sat down with a thump next to Suraj and eyed his plate hungrily.

Shiv stood up and announced that he was off to the

fields. In a moment, he had disappeared.

Tara continued cooking, knowing that a few extra chappatis would be needed for their lunch.

"That's mine," whined Suraj.

Tara looked up. Layla had stuffed a bit of Suraj's chappati in her mouth and was chewing furiously.

"You greedy pig," whispered Tara glaring at Layla. "I'm not going to give you any more."

Layla was Kali's daughter from a previous marriage. Being an only child, she had been pampered and spoilt. Her only hobby was eating and, at seven years old, she resembled a baby buffalo, with a temperament to match.

Layla immediately burst into tears, an art she had perfected over time. She opened her mouth and bawled.

"MOTHER! Tara is not giving me any food."

Kali descended on them like a thundercloud. She seized Suraj by the ear and dragged him out of the kitchen. His eyes tearing with pain, Suraj followed her meekly. Kali then turned on Tara and pushed her out of the kitchen with a violent shove.

"OUT! Get out. You should be *ashamed* of yourself, starving your little sister."

"But she ...," started Tara.

"Shut up," snarled Kali. "Not another word out of either of you. Get out of my sight."

Smarting at the injustice, Tara and Suraj walked out into the weak November sunshine to do their numerous chores. She had gone hungry yet again and Suraj had eaten but two or three morsels of food. Not enough for a growing boy. How would they survive at this rate?

She had to weed and water the tiny vegetable patch in the front of their house, which gave them a meagre supply of tomatoes, beans, and okra — invaluable when food was scarce due to drought. Suraj had to scrub the soot-encrusted vessels with coconut husk. Before he went, he hugged Tara.

"Don't look so sad, Didi. Are you hungry? Shall I steal some food for you?"

Tara shook her head, too choked to speak. Suraj saw her expression and hugged her even tighter.

"Ask me a riddle, Didi. Come on; let's see if I can guess the answer."

"Suraj, I'm all right, really."

"Please, Didi. It's been ages since you asked me a riddle."

Tara gave a weak smile at the obvious effort that Suraj was making to cheer her up. He knew she loved riddles. Parvati and she used to have competitions all the time, and they kept a tally of who would solve the most riddles in the shortest time.

"Okay, Suraj. Now think carefully, because this is an easy one. Ready?"

Suraj nodded.

"It goes in green
White stones grind it

It comes out red
In a stream ... mind it!"

Suraj screwed up his face in mock concentration and Tara's eyes sparkled.

"Come on, Suraj, it's easy," she teased.

Kali came to the back door and bellowed, "You two are still here? Did I not tell you to get on with your work?"

She spat a bright red stream of betel nut juice in a corner near the door, swivelled on her heel, and went in. Tara looked at the juice and looked at Suraj, her eyes dancing.

"Paan," sang out Suraj, referring to the betel nut juice that Kali had just spat out.

Tara tousled his hair.

"You're lucky that witch came out when she did, or you'd never have guessed."

Suraj smiled and skipped off to do his chores. Tara turned to her task, her anger not yet forgotten. *Why, Lord Ganesh? Why are you letting this happen to us?*

She could handle the abuse that Kali put them through, but her heart went out to her little brother. Day by torturous day she could see his animated spirit being subdued by this spiteful woman. His laughter was less frequent, his silent spells longer.

We have to escape, she thought as she savagely uprooted plants and weeds alike and threw them into a straw basket.

There was a time when she believed her father would stand up to her stepmother, but she no longer had faith in him. Kali's intolerable cruelty had chipped away at their happiness and confidence. "Stand up for yourself. Fight for what you believe in," her mother had always said.

Tara remembered the one time when she had tried to stand up to Kali. After a hard slap and having to miss meals for a whole day, she never tried again.

Escape to another village far away was their only hope. She would have to plan it well. Winter in the Kalesar forest would be harsh. The dangers were many: wild beasts, the intense cold, and other "things" that inhabited the forest.

Rumours abounded in Morni about strange monsters that attacked people in the forest. Someone had called them "Vetalas" (meaning "ghosts"), and the name had spread like wildfire to all the surrounding villages. They would have to escape as soon as possible and find a safe and dry place to spend the winter while they decided where they could go. She knew of a number of villages nestled on the other side of the hills.

If only they could cross the hills, they would be safe.

CHAPTER 3
KHEER TO DIE FOR!

"People of Morni, the Panchayat have an announcement. Come now."

The announcer ran past Tara's hut. She immediately abandoned the weeds and stood up. Suraj was already by her side. Hand in hand, they followed the crowd to the banyan tree in the village centre to be closer to the Panchayat. Tara had a feeling this was going to be a very important announcement. "Kamlaji," Tara addressed her neighbour respectfully, "do you know what's going on?"

"No," said the lady, quickening her step before Tara could ask another question.

Tara looked at the receding back with an ache in her heart. Kamlaji had been a lot friendlier when her mother had been around. Once again her lips moved involuntarily, in prayer for her mother's return.

They reached the banyan tree and sat down close to the raised platform that encircled it.

Raka and the four elders that made up the village Panchayat were already seated in a semi-circle, looking grim. As soon as everyone had settled down, Raka began without any preamble.

"I saw the mor this morning. The bird came at dawn and danced for a long time before it disappeared."

"Are you sure?" asked a wizened old man who appeared to be a hundred years old.

Raka nodded.

"What does this mean, seeing a peacock?" asked a villager. "I thought seeing a peacock was a thing of joy. It's a beautiful bird, no?"

"Not in this case," answered Raka. "Our village is named after the peacock for a reason. As legend goes, whenever Morni is in danger, a peacock comes to the village and warns us. It has been so long since Morni has been in danger that the legend was forgotten ... until today!"

"You've seen a peacock's tail, haven't you?" asked Raka.

The villager nodded, looking perplexed.

"Have you noticed that the circles on its tail resemble eyes?"

The villager raised his eyebrows. "I never thought of it that way."

"The mor is called 'the bird of a hundred eyes,'" said Kartik, one of the Panchayat.

"And this is a warning that we have to keep our eyes open. Danger is approaching ... or already here," said Raka.

"I have heard that the Vetalas have been sighted at Ropar, not too far from us. Be very careful when going to the forest. Don't venture there alone and never go after dark. Is that clear? Now, go back to your chores."

Everyone looked worried. There was a moment of silence. The villagers dispersed while the Panchayat continued chatting. Tara was slow to get up and heard one of the men say, "It was good of you to warn the villagers about the Vetalas, Raka."

"What have we decided about Zarku?" asked another member of the Panchayat.

The word "Zarku" made Tara's skin crawl. She gave Suraj a little push.

"Go on home, Suraj. I have something important to take care of," she whispered.

Suraj opened his mouth to say something, but Tara's expression shut him up.

"Yes, Didi," he said and ran off.

Tara circled the tree to the spot directly behind the Panchayat and squatted below the platform so that she could hear them unseen.

"It is odd that he turns up from nowhere and knows the affairs of our village so accurately," said Varun.

"It seems like he has an informer inside Morni," said Raka. "Have Dushta bring Zarku here."

Kartik called out to a passing villager, asking him to convey the message to Dushta. The villager returned with Dushta — a short man with oily black hair parted down the middle. His eyes had a shrewd look in them as if constantly searching for the opportunity to make money. His hand alternated between stroking his pot belly and rubbing his thumb and forefinger together.

"What are you doing here?" snapped Raka. "We asked Zarku to present himself."

"My respected elders," said Dushta, folding his pudgy hands. "Zarku wishes to speak with Raka, after which he will present himself in front of the Panchayat."

Raka looked annoyed at being counter-summoned. He got off the platform and strode off in the direction of Dushta's hut. Dushta sat down on his haunches next to the others to wait. A long time passed and the remaining members of the Panchayat were starting to get restless.

"What is happening?" one of them said. "Why is Raka taking so long? We should investigate."

No sooner were the words out of his mouth when they saw Raka striding back. He reached the group and announced, "I have had a long chat with Zarku. I believe that he is an accomplished healer and much better than Prabala."

Everyone gaped at him. Tara felt a jolt in her chest at the words. *Morni was going to replace her grandfather*. She had to bring him back.

"Raka, are you sure?" asked one of them.

"I am sure," he said in an expressionless voice. "I want no further discussion or argument."

"In that case, we should give him Prabala's hut and

make a formal announcement to the village," said Kartik.

"Yes, we should do that as soon as possible. Send messengers throughout the village and let them rejoice that Morni has a new, more powerful healer," said Raka.

They all dispersed and, a few seconds later, Tara crept away.

• • •

As soon as Tara got back, she continued with weeding the vegetable patch. Suraj was nowhere to be seen. Raka's words echoed in her mind. Morni was in danger and Prabala was gone. Now Zarku would replace him. It was not fair. Her grandfather had done so much for the villagers. The least they could do was wait for him to come back or send someone to find him. He was alive and so was her mother. She knew it in her heart.

Two thin arms encircled her neck.

"Didi, I worked really hard and made all the vessels gleam, so Mother told me I could go and play till lunchtime, so I came to help you," Suraj said, all in one breath.

Tara stood up and hugged Suraj, feeling her throat tighten.

"Thank you, Suraj. If you finish weeding this patch, I'll wash the clothes in the back. Then we can leave a bit earlier to feed Father."

Suraj squatted on his haunches immediately, his small, brown hands tugging at the weeds. With a last look at him,

Tara went to the back of the house, collecting a pile of dirty clothes along the way.

As the sun climbed higher in the sky, Tara scrubbed and beat the clothes into cleanliness and hung them to dry on a string in the backyard. The water was all used up but she was too tired to get some more. A cot resting against the backyard wall beckoned to her but she knew rest was impossible. It was time to take father his lunch. She decided to pack a few extra chappatis so they could all eat together.

"Didi, I'm done," sang Suraj, skipping toward her.

"Shhhh! If Mother hears you, we'll both get more chores," said Tara. "Fill a pot with water to take, and wait for me."

Suraj pinched his lips shut and did as he was told. Tara tiptoed into the kitchen. Kali was in the front room, gossiping with a neighbour and sipping a cup of tea. Noisy slurping and hushed voices reached her ears. Layla was nowhere around. She grabbed a few chappatis and packed them into a steel plate with some leftover vegetables and dabs of mango pickle. She covered the meal with extra plates, tied a clean cloth around the package, and crept out stealthily.

Suraj was waiting for her in the backyard. Sneaking backward glances, they raced toward the banyan tree. Their father's fields were on the far side of it.

As they reached the clearing, they saw a group of people standing and talking in hushed voices. A woman stood to one side, sobbing. Tara slowed down.

The woman's sobs grew louder. Keeping her head down, Tara walked past as slowly as she could. She gestured to Suraj to slow down as well. He stuck his tongue out at her but did as he was told.

"Shakti, oh my dear husband Shakti," wailed the woman, sitting on the ground, beating her chest with the palms of her hands. A couple of women passing by stopped to comfort her.

"He went out yesterday to catch hares for our dinner," she sobbed. "He has still not returned. Someone please bring my husband back to me."

The men walked out of earshot of the women. Tara followed them, straining her ears.

"What happened? When did he disappear?" asked one villager.

"Yesterday," replied another. He frowned and raised his head, staring into the distance. All the men followed his gaze to the Shivalik Hills. The dense forest that covered their slopes came right up to the edge of their village.

"Did Raka send a search party?"

"Yes. All they found were his slippers and his lantern. There seemed to be some black liquid and a bit of blood on the ground near the peepul tree not too far from here."

"Sister, don't cry," said one of the men returning to the sobbing woman. "We will find him."

They walked off and Tara heard no more. But she knew it was serious. Rakaji had just warned them all about the Vetalas. Men were disappearing into the forest from the other villages, never to be seen again. Shakti was the first from Morni.

And Tara was contemplating running away. Was she mad? Were they destined to starve at the hands of Kali, or should she take her chances and escape? Her head ached trying to decide. What should she do?

"*Come on*, Didi, what are you waiting for?" said Suraj, tugging at her sleeve. "I'm so hungry."

Tara nodded and sped up.

•••

They ran all the way to their father's fields, where rice and wheat crops undulated in a green ripple, stirred by a faint breeze. Shiv was still working in the fields and Tara saw a brown speck moving in the sea of green in the distance.

"Go run and get him," said Tara, giving Suraj a gentle push. "I'll unpack the lunch."

Suraj sprinted toward Shiv, a blur of dark brown darting between the lush green paddy. By the time Tara had divided up the food into three plates, her father and Suraj had arrived.

Tara held out a glass of water, which her father took without a word. After splashing his face, gargling, and drinking the rest, he sat down in the shade of the tree and pulled his plate toward him. Tara and Suraj started eating.

Only the harsh cry of a crow disturbed the afternoon.

No one spoke. Tara stared at her father, each bite sticking like a bit of coal in her throat. *Where are you, Father? Why won't you talk to us anymore?* At that moment her father glanced up at her. Tara stared at the brown eyes that had once brimmed with love. Now they resembled a dried-up well. *It's almost like Lord Yama, the God of Death, visited you, Father. He took your soul but he forgot to take your body.*

They all continued eating steadily and within a short while the plates were clean. Shiv washed his hands and then lay down under the tree for a nap.

"Didi, we don't have to go home right away, do we? There's an anthill I want to explore."

His sparkling eyes and smile, as rare as the peacock she had sighted, were too much to resist.

"All right, Suraj. But you have an hour or so at the most. Okay?"

He nodded and zipped away.

Tara lay down a distance away from Shiv, gazing at his face. He had not spoken a word to them all afternoon. She could remember the time when he spoke so much, especially the stories he told them. She had been fascinated by the one about Lord Yama when he came to claim Satyaban, the young prince. She loved the way Savitri outwitted the God of Death.

Tara put an arm over her eyes to block out the sunbeams dancing between the shimmering leaves. From the depths of her memory, the strong deep voice of her father washed over her.

"In the days of old it was said that there lived a beautiful princess named Savitri, the daughter of King Aswapati of Madra Desa. She was unparalleled both in virtue and beauty. Her father was unable to find a suitable husband for her, and so she was given complete freedom to choose her own. With a band of wise ministers she traveled to many countries but couldn't find anyone she wanted to spend her life with. While returning home through a jungle, a handsome young man cutting wood caught her eye. The young man was none other than Satyaban, a prince in exile who was living in the forest with his blind parents. Savitri selected him as her husband. But Narada, a musician and sage, forecasted that he would die young."

Tara felt her pulse quicken even now, as it had then, whenever she heard about "death." Her father's voice continued.

"The king pleaded with his beloved daughter to select another husband. But Savitri was firm in her decision and ultimately married Satyaban. She left the palace and lived with her husband and in-laws in the forest. As a devoted wife and daughter-in-law she looked after them very well. Gradually, the ordained time for Satyaban's death drew near. One day, while cutting wood in the jungle, he fell into a swoon and died, his head cradled in the lap of his beloved wife."

A sharp stone dug into Tara's shoulder blade. She shifted her weight, closed her eyes, and drifted back to her father's soothing voice as he continued the story.

"As Savitri sat weeping, she saw a large, green man astride a red bull come up to her. He towered well over Savitri and carried a mace. He was Lord Yama, the God of Death. He told Savitri that he had come to take her husband away. She refused him and clung to Satyaban's body. Lord Yama lifted Satyaban's body, put it on the bull, and rode away. Sobbing, Savitri followed. He could hear the silvery tinkle of her anklets as she followed him toward Taksala, the Gates of the Underworld.

"'Go back, Savitri. You cannot get your husband back,' said Lord Yama.

"'I cannot leave him, my Lord,' she answered.

"'I will grant you three wishes. Ask for anything but your husband's life,' said Lord Yama, taking pity on a woman who was widowed at such a young age.

"For her first wish, she asked that her father-in-law regain his kingdom. For her second wish, Savitri asked that her in-laws be granted their eyesight. Lord Yama granted both her wishes immediately," Shiv's voice, warm and full of love and wisdom, continued.

At this point, Tara remembered, she had put her head in her father's lap and he had stroked her hair. She felt her chest tighten.

"'You have one more wish. Ask for anything but your husband's life,' said Lord Yama.

"'I wish to be the mother of a hundred sons,' said Savitri promptly.

"'Granted,' said Lord Yama, equally promptly.

49

"Then he realized what had happened and he smiled at her cleverness. Savitri's religion did not allow a widow to remarry and Satyaban's soul was in his hands. He had no choice but to restore him to life to fulfill the third wish he had granted Savitri. Lord Yama, in spite of being outwitted, was moved by Savitri's devotion. Satyaban came back to life again and both of them lived happily ever after."

Tara awoke to a harsh caw and felt something wet on her forearm. She sat up. Was it raining? There was not a cloud in the sky. She felt her face. Her cheeks were wet. She shot a glance to where her father lay. The spot was empty.

She dragged herself up with a deep sigh. She had dozed off and it was late in the afternoon. She would get an earful from Kali, she was sure of that. Calling a reluctant Suraj to her, they gathered the empty dishes and headed home as fast as they could.

As they entered the hut they braced themselves for a torrent of abuse.

Silence.

"Tara, Suraj, you're back already? Come here my children," called out Kali in an unrecognizably sweet voice.

Tara and Suraj looked at each other in amazement.

"Is that Mother?" he asked in surprise. "I've never heard her speak this way to us. Do you think she loves us all of a sudden, or has a demon possessed her?"

Tara shook her head and shushed him as they entered the kitchen. Kali sat in front of the fire preparing dinner.

To one side of the stove lay an open vessel that gave off the most delicious fragrance.

"Mother, is that rice kheer?" asked Suraj, smacking his lips.

"Yes, Suraj. Let me put it outside to cool and then you can have some. I made it especially for you and your sister. I have been very bad tempered lately due to my ill health. I thought I would make it up to both of you," she said, smiling.

She looked like a jackal grinning at the sight of a meal. Tara shivered. Why was Kali doing this?

"Come sit by me, Suraj. Tell me what you did today," said Kali, still using that sugary-sweet voice.

Tara walked out to the backyard to complete her chores. Unease churned inside her stomach. As she cleaned the yard and sprinkled water to settle the dust, the village stray dog, Moti, wandered in. He looked starved as usual. Engrossed in her thoughts, Tara did not pay any attention to him as he roamed their backyard sniffing at various things and occasionally urinating. In the kitchen, Suraj still chattered away about their morning.

A shrill voice piped in, "Mother I want some kheer. I'm hungry."

"No, Layla. This is only for Suraj and Tara."

Tara stiffened in surprise. Layla refused food on their account? Something was very, *very* wrong. She stood in the courtyard chewing her lower lip. Something was going to happen! But what?

In the meantime, Moti had circled the courtyard and stopped outside the kitchen door where the fragrance of the cooling kheer on the back step beckoned to him. He looked around furtively and, seeing no obstacle to a free meal, he put his face into the vessel and lapped up the kheer.

The instant Tara took a step forward to drive him away, an image of Lord Yama astride his bull exploded in her mind. She stood paralyzed. What did it mean? Her mind went round in circles. She stood still and watched as Moti lapped up the kheer with great haste. Within minutes it was gone and Moti slunk off.

Tara continued sweeping and the image faded away, like a strong wind through wisps of smoke. Scared and extremely puzzled, she tried to sort out the thoughts in her mind. Why did she see that image?

"Hai Ram! Who ate the kheer?" shrieked Kali.

Tara snapped out of her reverie. She looked up and saw Kali at the back door, hands on her waist, her face like a thundercloud. Kali narrowed her eyes and her huge bosom heaved.

"Tara, did you eat it?" she yelled.

Tara put down her broom and walked toward Kali.

"No, Mother," she said with a straight face. "I was sweeping the yard."

"LAYLA," Kali screeched. "Come here."

This should be fun, thought Tara. It was not often their stepsister was yelled at.

"Yes, Mother," said Layla as she came running from the front room where she had been playing with her dolls. One was still tucked under her arm.

"Did you eat the kheer when I told you not to? I had left it out here on the back step to cool and now it's gone."

"No, Mother."

A giggle escaped her, which seemed to infuriate Kali. She shook Layla hard.

"Are you sure you didn't eat any?" she demanded.

Layla shook her head and Kali exhaled noisily.

Suraj stood cowering behind Tara. He had been with Kali all the while and was spared her wrath.

"Mother, why are you so angry? I am sure we can make some more kheer. What was so special about it anyway?" asked Tara, observing Kali very closely.

Kali turned pale and sweat stood out on her forehead. She dabbed it in quick, jerky movements with a trembling hand. Large patches appeared at her armpits and rapidly spread on her blouse, giving off an acrid smell.

"You STUPID girl! It took a lot of time to make. I thought you ungrateful children would appreciate the effort. Instead, the kheer has disappeared and no one knows who ate it. Hai Ram ... what liars I am surrounded with."

Kali glared at the three children as they looked up at her innocently and slightly puzzled.

Suddenly, a loud and agonized howl rent the air. Kali clapped her hand to her mouth, eyes darting right and left.

Tara, Suraj, and Layla looked at her and then all of them turned and raced in the direction of the howl.

Moti lay at the edge of their yard, thrashing his head and uttering the most heartrending howls of agony. Green froth drooled from his mouth, gathering in a pool in the dust, and his body jerked in spasms. Within seconds his yelps and howls became weaker as he succumbed to the intense pain that racked his thin body. Finally, his head lolled and he lay still. They all rushed closer. Even in the fading light of the evening it was unmistakable. Mixed in that green vomit were undigested grains of rice.

Tara looked up in horror.

CHAPTER 4
DIVINE HELP

"Why are you looking at me like that?" screamed Kali, her face the colour of soured milk.

"Moti ate the kheer and died. This kheer was made especially for *us*," screamed Tara. *To kill us*, completed the small voice inside her.

"Don't be ridiculous," stammered Kali. "You're talking nonsense! This rabid dog must have eaten some rotten food and died. It had nothing to do with the kheer. Anyway, who says he ate the kheer I made?"

"I saw him," said Tara, staring at Kali.

The venom in Kali's eyes shocked her. Tara gathered a bewildered Suraj to her and walked off.

"I'm going to tell Father about this," Tara called over her shoulder, trying to put as much distance between them as possible.

Kali strode behind Tara. She grabbed hold of Tara's plait and jerked her around till she was face to face with her.

Black eyes bored into soft brown ones.

"You will do nothing of the sort," Kali hissed. "One word from you and I'll make both your lives more miserable than they already are. Remember that."

Tara looked deep into those pitiless eyes and believed her. Kali released Tara, went back into the hut, and slammed the door shut.

I'll pay you back one day, thought Tara, rubbing her aching scalp. *My day will come.*

That night, as she lay tossing and turning on the thin mattress, Tara's thoughts were very troubled. This was a very close call and there was a sinking feeling in her stomach that this attempt on their life was not the last. *Nor the first*, the small voice piped in. She shivered and gathered Suraj closer to her.

"Didi, why does Mother hate us so much? What have we done wrong?" he whispered in her ear.

Tara heard the deep fear and hurt in his voice.

"I don't know, Suraj."

There was no point in lying. The more aware they were of danger, the greater their chances of survival.

"I was so happy when she had made the kheer for us. It felt like our real mother was back. But she was only trying to get rid of us forever. I'm so scared," he said.

His voice broke and he buried his face in her shoulder, sobbing softly.

Tara closed her eyes and took a deep breath to hold back the tears that threatened to break through her fragile self control. *I'm scared too,* she thought, *but who can I tell?*

Trying to keep her voice steady she replied,

"I wish that too, Suraj. But we have to look after ourselves till our real mother comes back. I made a promise to her. And she will be back. I'll bring her back — I will!"

She looked deep into her brother's eyes, trying to make him believe.

"Promise me that from now on you will not eat anything that witch gives you. Only what I feed you. Promise me, Suraj, no matter how hungry you are."

"I promise, Didi."

"Good. Now go to sleep and let me think. We have to escape as soon as possible. As long as I am here, I'll not let anything happen to you."

She smiled at Suraj. He nestled his face against her shoulder and fell asleep, tears still glistening on his thin cheeks. Tara wiped them away gently and cuddled him.

Her mind was a jumble of questions that whirled and bounced around, making her head ache. *Should we tell someone in the Panchayat, or should we escape to the forest and take our chances with the wild animals?*

On the one hand, the villagers were scared of Dushta the moneylender and his daughter, Kali. Who would side with two children?

But what if they chose to escape to the forest, and Suraj was killed by wild animals? What if she was killed and he was left all alone? And on and on and on. The decision was hers to make.

Her merciless mind pounded her with questions, each one landing like a sledgehammer on her heart. She tossed and turned as her body responded to the writhing of her agonized mind.

Mother, where are you? Tara thought. In her mind's eye she saw the beautiful Parvati, daughter of Prabala, the most powerful healer in all of India. He was a guru in Ayurveda and blessed by the gods for his intense meditation.

"Mother, if only I could see into the future like you can, I'd know what to do," sighed Tara.

Tara sat up, too unhappy to sleep. She checked to see if Suraj was asleep and then, making sure that the thin sheet was snug around him, she tiptoed to the kitchen for a drink of water. She eyed the heavy black skillet that lay on the blackened bricks longingly. One hard smack on her head and she would sleep till morning; unconsciousness was also a kind of sleep! She shook her head at her silliness and poured herself water from the earthen pot. The familiar fragrance of wet clay wafted up and she inhaled deeply, feeling a slight sense of calm.

As she sipped water from the glass, she opened the back door for some fresh air and shivered as a cold draft rushed in. She sat down on the doorstep and stared up at a sky awash with stars.

"What am I to do, Mother? Father is useless! Wherever you are, please hear me ... help me."

She heard her mother's voice in her mind, almost as if she were sitting next to Tara, whispering in her ear.

"Whenever you need help, Tara, pray to Lord Ganesh. He helps those in trouble and removes the most insurmountable obstacles. Go to his temple and make an offering."

Tara jumped up. Why hadn't she thought of it before? She tiptoed to the main room and arranged her pillow under the sheet next to Suraj so no one would notice her absence. Then she crept back into the kitchen and filled a small bowl with sugar to take as an offering to Lord Ganesh. She draped an old shawl around her and silently walked out the back door.

The forest was wide awake. Owls hooted and bats zoomed overhead like black shadows. She heard the steady drone of insects and lizards on their nocturnal forages. Occasionally she heard a deep roar of a tiger and the squealing of a wild pig.

Surrounded by these familiar sounds, she jogged along the path to the temple a short distance away, a full moon lighting the way. The wind rustled through the trees and the shadows stirred around her. She was quite at peace till she heard the sound of feet behind her.

Tara's heart leapt to her throat. She looked back, straining to see who it was. The road was empty. She sensed something or someone following her and started running. Her leather shoes slapped against the packed mud road as she sprinted for the safety of the temple, looking around her. Shadows moved and melted into each other. She smelt a foul smell, like the time a rat had died in their house.

"Lord Ganesh, look after me," she prayed as she ran.

Thankfully, the footsteps did not follow her up the temple steps. Tara bounded up and stepped through the wooden doors, gasping for breath. On a dais was a large clay figure of a man with a pot belly. The head was that of an elephant. Colourful clay jewels adorned the bare chest and a beautiful crown with multi-coloured stones graced the elephant's head. Smudges of vermillion powder lay on the forehead and tusk of the deity. He had four hands, each holding a different article. Tara stepped forward and poured the sugar in a small white mound at the feet of Lord Ganesh. She kneeled and whispered a prayer.

"Give me strength, my Lord. What should I do?"

A spitting, hissing sound roused her. She sat up and looked around. In the dim room lit by small clay lamps she saw a cat pawing at something in a corner. Tara picked up a lamp and walked to the back of the room. A small black ball of fur was quivering in the corner: a mouse! The cat pawed and hissed at it. The mouse bared his teeth and then cowered as the cat moved closer.

"Shoo," said Tara, waving her hand. The cat turned and glared at her with jaundiced eyes. It was a dirty grey, and painfully thin. The mouse emitted a pathetic squeak and the cat turned its attention back to it, ignoring Tara.

"Shoo," she said again, raising her voice. Balancing on her left foot she slipped off a mojri from her right foot. She brandished it and advanced on the cat.

"Get away, go" she snarled in a low, yet firm, voice and waved the shoe convincingly. The cat spat at her and then slunk away. The mouse was still quivering in the corner. Tara reached out for the bundle of fur. The mouse allowed her to lift him onto her palm. She raised it to eye level and mouthed softly,

"You're safe now, little mouse. Go home to your family."

Tara shook her head. *I have no one to talk to and now I'm talking to a mouse.* The mouse was looking at her earnestly. She lowered her palm to the floor and slid the mouse off it. It streaked to the hole at the foot of the deity and disappeared from sight. Tara put on her shoe and returned to her kneeling position in front of the statue.

"I helped your companion escape today, Lord. Please give us your blessings for our escape."

It was well-known that a mouse was supposed to be the faithful servant and companion of Lord Ganesh.

Tara touched her forehead to the clay feet one last time and, shuffling backwards to the entrance so that she did not offend the Lord by showing her back to him, she exited the temple.

Outside, she searched the shadows, her heart thumping against her ribcage. She saw no one as she ran down the steps and sprinted home.

As she neared the back door of their hut, she heard voices. Tara stood absolutely still in the shadows, and strained to hear the conversation.

"Fool woman. You have failed yet again," said a deep voice.

As the voice washed over Tara, she felt as if she was caught in a nasty thunderstorm with needles of ice-cold rain piercing her flesh. It sounded familiar. Where had she heard it before?

"Forgive me, Master, I am trying my best," a woman's voice replied in a grovelling tone. "But why can't you help me?"

Kali! Tara shivered. What had that witch failed to do? And who was she talking to in the middle of the night?

"Shut up, you worthless lump. I have more important things to do. The children must be dead and *soon*. And," he continued in an icy tone, "no one must suspect I have had a hand in this. I must see them while their flesh is still warm."

"But why?" asked Kali.

"One drop of their blood, one tiny bite of their flesh, and I will have partaken of Prabala's flesh and blood as they are his grandchildren. It will be harder for him to harm me. Do you understand?"

"Yes," said Kali.

"Ruin my plans, woman, and you will die a very horrible and painful death," the cold voice continued.

"One chance is all I ask for. Shiv will be going to Ropar this Sunday. I will have all day to carry out your command. This Sunday, Tara and Suraj will be dead."

Tara almost gasped out loud. Kali and an unknown man were plotting to kill Suraj and her! Now she understood why Kali had made the kheer. She clenched her teeth to stop them from chattering. Bile rose in her throat and she had to swallow hard to stop it from flooding her mouth. Black spots danced in front of her eyes. They had three days to live before Kali carried out her evil plan.

"Till Sunday, then. I will return at midnight. You had better have two corpses to show me. Don't forget, you have everything today because of me. I could take it away in the *blink of an eye*," said the voice.

Tara stood still as she heard footsteps crunch and fade into the night. Kali went back into the house. Tara forced herself to wait till Kali fell asleep. The cold and the fear of what she had heard made it unbearable. After a long time, she slipped in quietly through the back door. Kali was snoring.

Should we run away right now? She had just extended her hand to wake Suraj when she thought about the Vetalas. Her courage melted away. One more night: they'd stay one more night and then they'd go. It would at least give her time to gather clothes, medicine, and food to survive in the forest.

If they didn't escape by Sunday, their fate would be sealed. Kali would see to it.

CHAPTER 5
ZARKU

Tara awoke with a start and sat up. A deafening crash of thunder followed a jagged scar of lightning. Missing the warmth of his sister's body, Suraj woke up, too. They hugged their knees to their chests and stared out through a crack in the window at the grey world beyond.

"Something happened last night, Suraj," whispered Tara, leaning close to her brother. "I must tell you about it. I'll make the tea. You go brush your teeth and come into the kitchen. Be quiet now. We don't want to wake anyone."

Suraj yawned, scratched his head, and stood up. Everyone slept peacefully.

Tara rolled up the bedding quietly and stowed it in a corner of the room. They tiptoed into the kitchen. Suraj had gone out the back door and a cold gust of wind and rain swept into the room. Tara shivered. Within minutes she had a warm fire crackling and made tea for both of them. Suraj came back from the backyard, soaked, but wide awake and grinning.

Tara brushed and came back within minutes, cold but refreshed.

As soon as they'd finished breakfast of stale chappatis, Tara led Suraj to the far corner of the kitchen. They cradled their glasses of tea and sat with their backs to the wall to get a clear view of the front room.

"We have to run away, Suraj. At first light tomorrow!"

"Run away? But why?" asked Suraj in a shocked voice. "I don't want to go anywhere."

"So you'd rather stay here and be tortured?" snapped Tara.

Suraj's eyes filled with tears. "But where will we go? Who will look after us? And what if our real mother comes back? Will she know where to find us?'

"We'll go look for Mother and Grandfather. My heart says they are still alive."

Tara reached out and pressed her palm against Suraj's chest.

"What does your heart say?"

"Thump thump."

Tara smiled.

"That is your heart saying they are alive. Now, listen to me carefully: we have only today to gather everything we need."

Tara gazed into space, making a mental list of the things they would need. A small hiccup roused her. Tears streamed down Suraj's face and Tara put an arm around his shoulders.

"It will be safer than staying here. You trust me, don't you, Suraj?"

He nodded as a tear plopped into his tea. He wiped his face with his sleeve.

"If we leave at the first light tomorrow, we should be far away before anyone wakes up," she continued, speaking more to herself than Suraj.

Huddled close, they made a list of what they would need.

"Where will we collect our things, Didi? If we keep them anywhere in the house, the wicked witch will find them."

"I know what we'll do. We'll use a corner of Bela's shed. Kali never goes there. I am the only one who cleans her stall, anyway. Gather your clothes, some rope, a lantern, and matches and hide them under the jute sack I'll leave there. And Suraj, you must take extra clothing and stay dry at all times. You attract colds the way Dushta the money-lender attracts money."

They were so engrossed that they did not realize someone was towering over them till a voice boomed out.

"What is all this whispering about, you little cockroaches?" said Kali.

Tara and Suraj jumped.

"We were just talking about the ... uhhhh ... the ... rain," answered Tara, standing up and shielding Suraj, her eyes steady as they met Kali's.

The staring match continued for a while but Tara did not flinch. *Good girl*, said the little voice inside her. Their escape plan had made her realize that Kali had just one more day to bully them.

"Make some tea for your father and me," commanded Kali.

"Make it yourself," said Tara in a defiant voice before she could stop her herself.

Kali's eyes widened in surprise. She stepped forward, her hand raised to slap Tara, when Shiv stepped into the room. Kali lowered her hand.

"Father, can we go to the market today?" asked Suraj. "Please?"

Shiv thought for a moment, staring out the window.

"The fields will be flooded today. If the rain stops, I'll take you both," he said, nodding in their direction. "Come sit down. I'm sure Mother will not mind making tea for all of us this morning."

He patted the floor next to him. Kali glared at him but said nothing. She turned to the fire, her lips set in thin lines.

She will make us pay for this tomorrow, thought Tara. *Kali is not one to let any show of insubordination go unpunished. But we won't be here*, she thought to herself, and she smiled.

Her mind was busy with plans for the escape. While Shiv, Kali, and Layla finished their morning tea, Suraj and Tara excused themselves and went to the wooden cupboard in the front room. They rummaged through their belongings and clothes, smiling at each other whenever their eyes met.

"We'll both need an extra pair of shoes; these ones are falling to pieces. We'll need a couple of extra blankets, and reed mats to put on the ground when it rains." The list was endless and Tara was starting to think they would never be able to carry it all, Suraj was so thin and weak.

Tara searched for their warm clothes and her palm connected with something very soft. She pulled it out. It was her mother's favourite sky-blue kurta — the only piece of clothing left of her in the house. Had Kali found it, it too would have been burned with the rest of Parvati's clothes. Tara clutched it to her face, inhaling deeply. She was sure she could still get a faint whiff of the sweet lemony fragrance of the chameli flower. Suraj stepped closer as Tara held out the bunched-up garment to him. He buried his face in it and clutched her hand. For a moment, they felt that their mother was right there, embracing them.

"Tara, come here and clean up," hollered Kali.

Tara started. She was about to hide the kurta again when she heard a crackle. She scrunched up the kurta and heard it again.

"What is that sound, Didi?"

"Maybe a note Mother left us?" said Tara.

Her hands shook as she scrabbled through the left pocket, then the right, and extracted a ten-rupee note.

Suraj's eyes widened. He had never seen so much money.

"Ohhhhh," he breathed

"Thank you, Mother," said Tara in a soft whisper. "Don't tell anyone, Suraj."

She tucked the money into the pocket of her kurta and went back into the kitchen. There was a mess, as usual. Without stopping to acknowledge the annoyance and sense of injustice that rose in her whenever she had to clean up her stepmother's mess, she got to work.

Their father stepped out the back door to wash up. The rain had stopped and the sky had lightened to a smiling blue. A fresh breeze stirred the branches of the peepul trees lining the road and hundreds of droplets of water fell to the wet ground. Tara gazed out the back door. As far as the eye could see, vivid green trees swayed joyfully with their arms outstretched. All the dust and dirt had been washed away and the smell of damp earth wafted in.

"Hurry up, Tara, it's almost midday," said Shiv.

"Can I come too?" asked Layla.

"Hmmmm," said Shiv, and he stepped outside to smoke a beedi while he waited for his family to get ready.

Soon the kitchen was clean and the house tidy. The family walked toward the market. On holidays, the farmers and their wives congregated under the large peepul trees with their baskets of fruits and vegetables. The men smoked beedis, lamented about the weather and the state of their crops. The wives gossiped, admired each other's clothes, or swapped homemade cures.

The air was cold and clean and Tara inhaled deeply. In the distance, the Shivalik Hills towered over the village. Their tops were covered in clouds through which the sun peeped cautiously, as if playing hide and seek. Tara and Suraj walked hand in hand a little ahead of Shiv, Kali, and Layla. Tara looked up at the hills, and the lush green of the forest that covered the slopes. They looked dark and forbidding. Tomorrow, Suraj and she would be fighting their way through it.

"Mother, buy me some red bangles, please? I don't have any and my best friend has so many," pleaded Layla as they neared the market. Already there were a number of families milling around, enjoying the cool weather and the companionship.

"We're going to look around, Father," said Tara. "We'll meet you later at the bangle shop."

Her father nodded, not even looking in their direction. Tara felt a stab of hurt, which passed quickly.

Tara pulled Suraj in the direction of the cobbler.

"We both need a pair of waterproof shoes," said Tara.

She set off at a quick trot to the village cobbler on the far side of the market square, Suraj in tow. The cobbler's shop was a small, dingy hovel. There were mounds of shoes and chappals covering every inch of the floor except for the path that led from the door to the raised platform where he sat, like an impoverished king amidst his subjects. Footwear hung from hooks on the wall in every shade of brown and black, stitched with coloured embroidery. Other shoes sat patiently on shelves, covered with dust. A strong smell of uncured leather and glue hung about the room.

Occasionally a black furry ball moved in the depths of the shadows in the corners. The first time Tara had seen a movement she had screamed. Then she had realized what it was: big black rats that had made their home in the shop.

The cobbler sat in his workplace in one of the corners, thin and bent over, a posture acquired through years of hunching over the anvil. A grimy lantern hung from a cobweb-encrusted rope over the platform and threw feeble light on the shoe that he was repairing.

A woman balanced on one foot, her bare foot resting on the shoe-clad one, waiting for the shoe to be repaired. Tara decided to let her leave before approaching the cobbler. While they waited, she examined the mojdis and other types of shoes on display that were suited for all weather conditions in the mountains.

"Look here, Suraj, these shoes look sturdy. This one would fit me and that one looks just about right for you."

"They're too big," he said with a giggle.

"Don't worry; you can wear two pairs of socks. They'll be snug. We don't have time to get them made to order."

Fidgeting impatiently, Tara and Suraj anxiously peered out to check if Kali or Layla had seen them enter the shop. They were safe. There was no sign of their family. Finally, the woman departed. Tara stepped up to the cobbler before anyone else walked in.

"Baba," said Tara, addressing the older man with respect, "we would like to buy these shoes." She held out two sturdy pairs. They were made of dark brown leather with a pointed tip.

The cobbler looked up from his work and peered short-sightedly through glasses as thick as Tara's little finger. He stood up on the little platform and came toward them. Tara noted his shabby kurta and pyjama, which were patched up neatly with different bits of cloth and leather, like a colourful patchwork quilt. On his feet were a new pair of mojris. Tara smiled. He may not have been able to afford good clothes but his shoes were brand new.

"Tara! How are you and Suraj today? I have not seen you for ages. Not since your mother ..."

Seeing their expressions, he became silent

Tara swallowed the lump that suddenly formed in her throat.

"Our shoes are wearing out and Father told us to buy a new pair."

She hoped he would not see her flushed face as she uttered the lie.

"Very good choice, Tara," he said, looking at the shoes she had selected. "These are made from the hide of the Murrah buffalo. I have treated them with my special cream to make them waterproof."

He stroked the rich leather lovingly.

"Baba, these shoes are too big for my feet. Can you do something to make them smaller?" asked Suraj.

"Not to worry, my children, not to worry. Let me take your measurements and I'll make a pair that fits perfectly. You can have them in a week. Special rush job for you," he said, winking.

Tara got a whiff of onion and garlic on his breath as he leaned close.

"NO," said Tara, a bit louder than she had intended.

The cobbler leaned back in surprise and annoyance.

"All right, Tara. Calm down. You can have these now if you want them so badly."

He rummaged in the pile of scrap leather in front of him and pulled out some bits that matched the colour of the shoes. He handed them to Tara.

"Tuck these into the toe. Or put some strips near the heel. Wear thick socks and you'll be warm and comfortable. Good choice, lots of room for the toes to grow, henh?"

He chuckled and shuffled back to the platform.

Tara went up to him and held out the ten-rupee note. He looked up at her.

"I cannot take that, Tara. Your mother was like a sister to me. She always brought medicine for my aching eyes and never took a paisa from me. I *never* believed that she was a witch."

A sharp intake of breath stopped him from continuing.

"My mother, a witch?" whispered Tara. "Is that what people were saying? Is that why she ran away?" she asked in a softer voice, hands clasped at her chest.

"Yes, Tara. Most of the villagers thought she was a witch."

"But why?" asked Tara, tears welling up in her eyes. "All she did was warn people of danger and save their lives."

"Yes, but her foretelling powers scared some of the villagers. It is always the case when one cannot understand something. They fear it! Someone poisoned the minds of the Panchayat and they decided to stone her to death."

Tara turned pale. Beads of sweat stood out on her forehead and she was starting to feel nauseous.

"So that is why she had to go?"

"Yes, and Prabala went with her. He could not let his daughter brave the forest alone. Besides, he was very disappointed with the attitude of the villagers and decided to leave to teach them a lesson."

"But why did no one tell us anything?" asked Tara. "Even Mother did not say a word."

The cobbler sighed deeply.

"The Panchayat forbid us to speak of either of them again. And I think your mother did not want you to worry," said the cobbler.

Tara stared at the cobbler as thoughts churned in her head like a village-woman making buttermilk. The villagers thought her mother was a witch and they had wanted her dead. Was this the reason their father had married again? Why he hated them so much? Because they were the children of a witch? It was all too much to think about and she stood there dumbstruck. Someone tugged her kurta.

"Let's go, Didi. I want to go home," Suraj pleaded.

Tara saw the anguished look on Suraj's face.

"We must go, Baba," said Tara in as normal a voice as she could. "Thank you for the shoes," they said in unison, and hugged him.

He kissed their foreheads and then pushed them gently toward the door.

"Be careful, whatever you do. May Lord Ganesh be with you," he said.

Tara looked back at him in amazement. Did he know? But the cobbler was already engrossed in the next repair and did not look up. They walked out of the shop. Tara stuffed the shoes under her clothes and threw the red and blue shawl over her, hoping the bulge would go unnoticed till they reached home.

As they walked to the centre of the market, Tara noticed people whispering.

"Hai Ram, NOOOOOOOOO," a woman howled. "Oh my son, what has happened to you? Talk to me. *Say* something!"

The howling was coming from Ravi's hut. Ravi's old mother stood outside the door, beating her chest. Villagers who had been milling around rushed as one toward the wailing woman. Within moments a large crowd had gathered.

Tara and Suraj, on the outskirts of the crowd, craned their necks, but the crowd was too thick. Suraj got down on all fours and rapidly crawled between the sea of legs, drawn to the noise. Not wanting to miss a thing, Tara followed him. What she saw made her sit back in shock. Suraj had stopped too, and was crawling backwards and whimpering. He buried his head in his hands, trembling violently.

In the clearing lay Ravi, or what remained of him. His skin was an ugly shade of translucent green. Black liquid coursed visibly through his body. A black, fist-sized sack inflated and deflated in his chest. His eyes had rolled back in their sockets and he lay staring sightlessly at the crowd that pressed forward, gaping at him. His hair was matted and dirty. A foul stench emanated from his open mouth, as if something had died inside it. But what had the crowd shocked were his feet. They had turned 180 degrees, till his toes faced backwards. On his forehead was a deep gash from which oozed a black, viscous liquid. He drew in laborious gasps that sounded deafeningly loud in the pin-drop silence.

"Ravi, talk to me," pleaded his mother, sitting next to him but not daring to touch him.

A number of people tried to drag her away from that *thing* that lay on the ground. No one could understand what power could change Ravi into that deformed creature.

Tara clamped her lips shut to prevent her breakfast from spewing out. She crawled backwards and exited the crowd as fast as she could. *Who could have done this to Ravi?*

The muttering in the crowd rose to a crescendo.

"He went to the forest looking for firewood this morning," said someone.

"And then he was attacked. Could it be the Vetalas?"

"Looks like it. He came running home not a few minutes ago. He was conscious then."

"And he had the gash on his forehead. It was bleeding profusely. It looked like blood at first. Now it's this black liquid."

"And then he turned green and his feet rotated."

"What in the name of Lord Ram could do this to a person?" asked another shrill voice.

"We are all going to die. Someone call Raka. He will tell us what to do."

Confusion and panic abounded as someone ran to get the members of the Panchayat.

Raka came striding up to them. He looked calmly at the misshapen body lying on the ground. Tara just could not understand how he could be so unconcerned.

"What happened?" he asked.

The villagers told Raka what had happened while someone led Ravi's mother away from her son's deformed body.

"Call Zarku," said Raka calmly. "If anyone can cure Ravi, he can."

Another villager ran off for Zarku. He returned shortly, calling out, "Make way, make way for Zarku."

Tara saw a bald man in a long, flowing, black robe stride up to the crowd. This was the first time she had seen him since Diwali night.

His black eyes assessed the scene within seconds. They

rested on Tara and Suraj momentarily. Tara could feel hate and anger pulsing out at her and she was stunned. Why would this healer, who was so new to Morni, hate her so much? He passed her, and the crowd parted easily to allow him to walk up to the body. The crowd closed in behind him again so that Tara could not see what was happening. A low murmur reached her as she strained to hear what Zarku was saying. She grabbed Suraj's hand and pushed through the crowd till she could see Zarku's face and hear him as he examined the body.

"This is deep evil. Someone has put him under a spell and claimed his soul. Only I can free him. Bring him to my hut."

As soon as she heard his voice, a terrible fear clutched her heart. The voice she had heard last night, plotting with Kali to kill Tara and Suraj, was Zarku's. It was Zarku who wanted them dead. She wanted to run and hide, but she could not move.

The silence deepened. No one stirred. No one wanted to touch that monster. Ravi's heart continued beating, rising and falling with each ragged breath he drew in. Green spit drooled from the side of his mouth. Zarku looked at the crowd and his mouth curled at the corners.

"Will no one help me carry this man to my hut? He is one of your own. Surely a bit of deformity should not make him so repulsive to you?"

Silence.

There was an air of deep satisfaction on his face as he

looked at the stunned, scared faces around him.

"*You* are the evil one here," yelled a dishevelled young man, who broke through the crowd and rushed to Ravi's side.

"Mohan," said Raka in a stern voice. "We know Ravi was like a brother to you. But you cannot blame Zarku for what happened to him in the forest. Zarku is only trying to protect us. Get a hold of yourself and stop talking nonsense."

"No," said Mohan, shaking his head, wiping his streaming eyes and nose. "He is the cause of this, I know it. *I know it ...*"

"Thank the Lord that you have my protection," said Zarku as he strode forward and scooped up the body in both hands easily, as if he were picking up a child.

No one came forward to help him.

"No one is to enter my hut while I treat this boy," he said, his whiteless eyes sweeping the crowd. His gaze stopped on Mohan. Mohan returned his look defiantly. Then Zarku turned and walked away.

Tara and Suraj stood at the edge of the crowd as she watched the receding back of Zarku and noticed that Mohan was obediently shuffling behind him.

At that moment, Tara knew without a doubt: Morni was in very grave danger and they were running out of time. She had to brave the forest and reach the one place Prabala might be. She had to find him and bring him back!

CHAPTER 6
FREEDOM

"Let's go," Tara muttered to Suraj under her breath after Zarku had walked away.

Suraj was unusually quiet and very pale. Everyone looked the same. Murmurs and whispers spread through the crowd like ripples in a still lake.

"What happened to Ravi?"

"The Vetalas, they're here."

"What is going to happen to all of us if we cannot go to the forest? How will we get food and firewood?"

Unease hung in the air like a black cloud. The sky was a deep grey. People drifted away. Tara saw Shiv, Kali, and Layla in the distance. Her father had a deep frown on his face. Kali tried hard to maintain a blank expression, but her eyes sparkled and Layla played with her new bangles.

"Let's go home, everyone," Shiv said. "It has been a long day."

Tara was silent as she walked slowly behind her father. Suraj slipped a small, warm hand in hers. She raised an eyebrow.

"As long as we're together, Didi, I can be as brave as a lion. I will protect you," he said with a slight swagger in his walk.

Tara glanced at the scrawny body of her brother as he uttered the words and smiled. He looked more like a weak kitten than a lion.

"Thank you, Suraj," she answered him with utmost seriousness. "I love you. You know that, right?"

"I love you too, Didi. Even more than mangoes!"

Tara squeezed his hand. She saw the implicit trust in his eyes and made a promise to herself: *I cannot fail him! I have to take him to safety and back to our real mother.*

Suraj grabbed her hand and pointed.

"Look Didi — Dhruv Nakshatra, the North Star. Let's make a wish."

Tara closed her eyes and prayed in earnest.

"Lord Ganesh, keep us safe till we find Mother and Grandfather," whispered Tara.

"Didi, about Ravi," Suraj started to say.

"Shhhh, lets not talk about him. Not now," said Tara gently.

Darkness was seeping across the sky like an inkblot as lizards and crickets heralded the arrival of night. The sweet fragrance of the raat-ki-rani flower scented the air. Tara inhaled deeply.

Suraj stopped and scooped up something from the ground and straightened up.

"What is that?" asked Tara, suspicious of the mischievous glint that had suddenly appeared in Suraj's eye.

"Shhhhhh, watch!"

He quickened his step and reached Kali's large back, which swung like a pendulum as she waddled along. Suraj walked up close to her and gently placed a large greyish white lizard on the edge of her pallu, the part of the saree that was draped over her shoulder. He did it so carefully that Kali did not feel a thing.

He waited for Tara to catch up to him, his chest heaving with silent laughter. The lizard hung on to the edge of the saree, swaying precariously from side to side. In a blur of movement it shimmied up the remaining cloth and jumped onto the bare patch on Kali's shoulder. Kali felt the pattering of tiny feet and clapped her hand to her neck. Her heavy hand landed on the lizard's head and, dazed, it toppled forward into Kali's ample bosom. She felt it wriggle next to her skin. She gave a deafening shriek and desperately tried to shake the lizard out of her clothes.

Tara and Suraj had tears running down their faces as they tried to control the hysterical laughter that welled up within them at the sight of that huge mound of flesh, for once, engaging in an activity more strenuous than sitting. After a few minutes of furious groping down the front of her blouse, Kali managed to grab the wretched lizard in her pudgy hand and dump it unceremoniously on the road.

"Bloody lizard," swore Kali.

She glared at Tara and Suraj, who kept straight faces as they continued walking.

"Come on Kali, it was only a lizard," said Shiv. "You probably frightened it more than it frightened you."

A fresh wave of mirth went through Tara and she had to stuff her knuckle in her mouth to stop from giggling.

They reached home just as night fell. A cold wind had started up and they all hurried in and shut the door. Shiv lit the lantern while Tara groped her way into the kitchen to start dinner.

"Get all our things into the shed," Tara whispered to Suraj as she handed him their shoes in the semi-darkness.

He nodded and ran off.

"Call me as soon as dinner is ready," snapped a winded Kali, sitting on the cot trying to recover from the lizard encounter.

Tara got to work. Plans of their escape gave her a sense of hope that no amount of unpleasantness could extinguish.

When dinner was ready, Tara called everyone into the kitchen. Kali ignored them completely. Their father had gone out for a short while and returned with troubling news, which he shared with Kali and the children as they ate.

"Ravi is dead. Zarku could not save him."

"Did Ravi's family cremate him?" asked Kali.

"Apparently Zarku performed the last rites. He did not

want to upset Ravi's mother by showing her the deformed body again."

"That is odd, Father, isn't it?" asked Tara. "Only family members are allowed to set fire to the funeral pyre, not some stranger, even if he is the village healer. It is against tradition."

Her father frowned at her for interrupting.

"Mohon has disappeared. No one knows where he is," said Shiv as he tossed a ball of dal and rice in his mouth and chewed thoughtfully.

"Probably gone to the forest to seek out the Vetalas single-handedly, the fool," said Kali as she slurped her food.

For some time there was silence. No more was said about the disappearance, but Tara's stomach churned. Tonight was the last night they would have a roof over their heads. What would they find in the forest? Would she be able to find Prabala and her mother before the Vetalas found them? Her panicked mind darted about like a caged animal. Try as she might, she could not forget Ravi's mutilated body.

That night, when all were asleep, Tara and Suraj tiptoed into the kitchen and sat by the glowing embers of the kitchen fire.

"Is everything in the shed?" asked Tara. "I've made extra food. I'll pack it and put it into the bundles with a few more things we're going to need, especially medicinal herbs."

"Yes, Didi. Can we sleep now?" said Suraj, stifling a yawn.

"Pay attention, Suraj, our lives will depend on how well-prepared we are."

Chastened, Suraj nodded and promptly propped his eyes open with his thumb and forefinger and goggled at her. Tara could not help but smile.

At long last they finished making the plans. Suraj was half asleep and Tara, too, was tired. They crept into the main room and lay down on the thin mat. Tara's mind was filled with questions and worries and sleep was a very long time coming.

• • •

Dawn arrived clad in a shawl of ice. A chilly wind seeped into the huts as the people of Morni snuggled deeper into their blankets. Goats, cows, and pigs huddled together in their shelters, seeking warmth.

Tara woke especially early, feeling as if she had not slept a wink. Her eyes burned and her head felt as if it was made of lead. The beginning of a massive headache was making its way toward her temples. They had already put on their warm travel clothes the night before. Tara flung her favourite shawl around her shoulders. She was ready.

It was still quite dark. A pale, pink dawn tiptoed along the edge of the horizon. Tara shook Suraj gently. When he was awake, she put a finger to her lips and gestured in the direction of the kitchen. He nodded, picked up his shoes, and padded out silently. Tara stood up and went to where her father lay sleeping. She touched his feet lightly.

"I'll miss you, Father," she murmured inaudibly. "But we're going to look for Mother and we will bring her back. We will be a family again."

Then, without a backward glance, she crept out to Bela's shed. Suraj was still rubbing the sleep out of his eyes.

"Let's go," Tara said. "The sooner we are out of here, the better."

She handed Suraj the smaller of the two bundles and slung the larger one onto her back. She filled an animal skin with water, and put some milk in a glass bottle. Bela nudged Tara with her cold, wet nose and Tara turned back to hug her, tears in her eyes.

"Take care, Bela. We'll be back soon. With Mother."

Brother and sister walked out of the hut as dawn, in a bolder shade of pink, strode out from the horizon to embrace them. They walked east through the deserted village, the quickest route to Morni Hills, beyond which lay the Shivalik Range.

Within the hour they would be out of the village and away from the home they had known all their lives. The huts thinned out as they neared the green band of forest land that lay at the foot of the hills. It grew darker. The trees blotted out the sky and it became colder. The pukka road disappeared and they stepped onto a rough path that led deep into the forest.

Suraj stopped at the edge of the forbidding green mass and looked back. The huts, the village, safety, and security lay behind while danger lay ahead. He looked into Tara's eyes. She nodded, holding his gaze.

"As long as we're together, we'll be all right," said Tara.

They plunged into the foliage, keeping a sharp eye out for any movement. Mynas, kingfishers, and koyals twittered in the trees, welcoming the morning as the pair walked deeper and deeper into the forest. The sun came out and golden rays filtered in through the dense canopies, creating freckles of light on the grassy floor. The air was thick with the sickly sweet smell of rotting leaves.

"Didi, I have to stop now, I am really tired," said Suraj after they had been walking for what seemed like hours. He sank down on a grassy hill. Tara was a few steps ahead. She turned around to chide him and screamed.

"Suraj, don't move!"

Suraj froze. The expression on Tara's face was one of absolute horror. She advanced slowly, her eyes fixed on a spot above his head.

"Python," she breathed, clutching her throat.

A large brown and white python was curled around a branch just above Suraj's head. Its small head swung a hair's breadth away. It slithered lower. Still lower. Tara could not breathe. Suraj tilted his head back and stared straight into the black beady eyes of the snake. Sensing movement, the python opened its powerful jaws and lunged toward Suraj's head.

Tara's and Suraj's screams echoed through the Kalesar Forest.

CHAPTER 7
IN THE KALESAR FOREST

Suraj ducked.

At the same instant, the python whipped backward on its branch. Suraj ran to Tara, shaking so hard that he stumbled twice before he reached her outstretched arms.

They both looked up. A black cobra had dug its fangs into the tender belly of the python. The python tried to coil itself around the cobra, but the cobra was too small and agile. In a flash of black it disappeared into the leaves.

Tara held her breath as the heavy python uncoiled itself and slithered over the branches, trying to follow the smaller, suppler snake. Without warning, the black cobra dropped on the python's head from above. The python tried to change direction but it was too late. In a lightning strike, the cobra's fangs sank into its head. The python writhed in the throes of death as venom coursed through its body. The cobra flew from side to side with the thrashing python, but held on. Within seconds it was over. The python gave a last spasm, slipped off the branch, and fell with a resounding thud onto the forest floor. The cobra, whose fangs were still buried deep in the python's head, fell with it.

Tara and Suraj stared at the fight, holding hands so tightly that their knuckles were white. Once the python fell, the cobra disengaged its fangs from the python's lifeless body and dragged itself wearily toward the thick undergrowth. Before it reached the bushes it looked back. It raised its hood and stood still for a moment, staring at the children intently, and then disappeared.

Tara pulled Suraj and they hurried away, further into the forest. In a few moments they were out of breath.

"We have to stop now, Didi," gasped Suraj. "I can't run anymore."

They had reached a small clearing where the trees had thinned out and sunlight filtered in. There was very little vegetation on the ground. Tara scanned the clearing for any sign of danger. Finding none, she sank down on the ground holding the stitch in her side and Suraj flopped down beside her.

For a few moments, they looked at each other in relief and silence. Tara undid the heavy bundle she carried and took out some chappatis, an onion, and some pickles wrapped in a dried banana leaf. She put the onion on a rock, smashed it with the heel of her palm, and peeled it. The pungent vapours from the onion made her eyes water and nose twitch. She wrapped onions and pickles in a chappati and handed it to Suraj. Then she made one chappati roll for herself. They chewed the food, listening to the sounds of the forest around them.

A koel cooed and was answered by another. A golden oriole rose from one of the trees and flew off, a fistful of sunset across a canopy of green.

"I'm thirsty, Didi. Did you bring any water?"

Tara handed him the animal skin.

"Drink sparingly, Suraj. We may have long to go before we find a stream."

"Today the wicked witch will have to do her own work," said Suraj, with a grin on his face.

"Yes," said Tara. "The queen must be waiting for her tea. Except today she'll have to make it herself. And bring the water from the well, and cook and clean."

"And wash the vessels," piped in Suraj. "Can you imagine how angry she's going to be when she discovers her two servants have run away?"

He's hit the nail on the head, thought Tara. *We were her servants, but now we are free.*

"We need to move on, Suraj. We have to find a safe place to spend the night."

The anxiety in her voice made Suraj look up from the anthill that he was prodding with a twig. Large red ants swarmed angrily to the top and spilled over the side. Suraj jumped back. He dropped the twig and ran up to her.

"Didi, what would you do if you had to carry on alone?"

Taken aback, she stared at him. He looked back at her with a serious expression.

"What do you mean?"

"What if I am not around, Didi? Can you carry on alone and find Mother and Grandfather? You must, Didi, with or without me."

"Don't say that, Suraj. I need you with me," said Tara in an anguished voice. "You're scaring me. Do you know something I don't?"

"I had a dream last night, Didi."

"And?"

"I saw you climbing a mountain with a strange boy."

"And where were you?"

"I was not there."

Tara lunged and hugged him.

"It was just a dream, Suraj. Dreams don't come true. We're going to do this together, you and I. Don't you want to find Mother and Grandfather and be a family again?"

Suraj nodded.

They marched steadily as the day blossomed to a bright afternoon and then drooped into evening. Tara was so hungry that it felt as if there was a huge, gaping hole where her stomach should have been. She was sure Suraj felt the same. They stopped under a large kaurnar tree whose red flowers stood out like bright drops of blood amongst the dark green leaves. A welcome carpet of red petals at the foot of the tree beckoned to them. Tara unpacked some food and they chomped hungrily.

"I have a surprise for you, Suraj."

"What Didi?"

With a flourish, Tara produced a small mango from the depths of the bag and held it out to him. The sparkle in his eyes was worth the effort she had gone to get it.

"Oh, Didi, I love you!" he said, jumping up to hug her.

Suraj peeled off the soft skin of the mango with his teeth and within seconds was biting into its sweet, orange flesh. A rivulet of juice made its way to his elbow and Tara watched, astonished, as Suraj licked it all the way from wrist to elbow.

"You dog! Stop doing that!"

Suraj continued sucking the seed that was now devoid of any flesh. At long last he stopped and buried it in the soil next to him. "Didi, how could I waste a single drop of this lovely, tasty ..."

Tara smiled. "Enough of this. Now wash up. Quick." A couple of squirrels zipped down the tree and sat, unafraid, a few feet away from them. Barking deer and antelopes passed by in a blur of brown and white. Where there were deer, there were larger predators. Tara packed up and soon they were on their way.

They trudged on, keeping a look out for animals and poisonous insects around them. Sal, peepul, and shisham trees formed a green, leafy umbrella through which the late-evening sun filtered. Tara's eyes scanned the forest, searching for a place to spend the night.

The weakening light and increasing cacophony heralded the approach of night. The gloom deepened and an occasional star peeped between the leaves. Tara's pulse raced. What if they had to spend the night out in the open? What if they were attacked by a wild animal? What if ...? Scary thoughts ran unchecked through her head. Her grip on Suraj tightened.

Suddenly, night was upon them. All around, the forest was starting to wake up, one lazy hoot and catcall at a time. Tara gripped Suraj's hand tighter. Hers was slippery with sweat. The total darkness was like a thick, black cloud that enveloped them completely. Even the stars had disappeared.

Sounds of shuffling, snorting, and howling surrounded them as jackals, hyenas, neelgai, and leopards woke up for a night of hunting. Tara and Suraj plodded on. Roots tripped them so that on more than one occasion they sprawled headlong into the undergrowth. Neither said a word as they stumbled forward in the darkness.

"Didi, why don't you light the lantern?"

"No! We'll only attract wild animals. It is better to remain under the cover of darkness and hope for the best."

They stumbled a few more feet when suddenly Tara saw something that made her heart leap. She squeezed Suraj's hand and he returned the squeeze. He had seen it, too: a small glow in the distance; probably some friendly villagers? They scrambled toward the light as quickly as they could.

"Be very quiet till I see who it is," said Tara as they drew nearer.

Their steps slowed as the light became stronger. A small fire burnt brightly in a clearing. A tall, powerfully built man in a black robe paced near the fire. He walked a few steps. Stopped. Listened. Then he started pacing again.

Tara and Suraj crept closer, crouched in the bushes at the foot of a tall sal tree, and peered through the branches. They could not see the man's face but the moment he muttered to himself, Tara knew.

"Late again," the man spoke quietly to himself. "I'll punish them for keeping me waiting."

The shuffling of many feet made him prick up his ears. Tara and Suraj huddled closer.

The tall man had stopped pacing and positioned himself such that the light fell on his stern face and made him look even more forbidding. He was facing Tara so that she finally got a clear look at his face. Suraj whimpered and Tara clamped a hand on his mouth. Her skin was tingling and covered with goose bumps. Zarku!

In the flickering light of the fire, the third eye on his forehead throbbed with a life of its own as if impatient to open and wreak havoc on whoever displeased him. He crossed his arms and waited.

A band of men shuffled into the clearing. The light reflected off their green bodies. Their skin was almost translucent. In their chests their hearts inflated and deflated in a steady rhythm. A criss-cross of blood-engorged veins ran up and down their bodies. Each man in the group had an ugly scar on his forehead. Tara shuddered.

Suraj closed his eyes and buried his face in Tara's shoulder. Tara was mesmerized with the horror of seeing so many of these creatures all at once. So these were the Vetalas.

The leader of the pack came forward. Sweat ran down his gaunt face, which was framed by filthy, matted hair. He saw the expression on Zarku's face and fell to his knees, quivering. He grunted pitifully and bowed several times.

"How many more men did you capture from the village of Pinjaur, Jeevan?"

Jeevan shook his head.

"None? Explain yourself."

The words hung in the air, like arrows stopped in mid flight.

Tara was stunned. Capture? *Capture*? That meant these creatures were actually *villagers*? Remnants of her undigested meal climbed in her throat. Tara swallowed hard.

With sign language and grunts Jeevan managed to signify that the village they had raided that night had sentries and dogs at the gate.

"Did you kill the dogs?"

Jeevan looked up in confusion. It was obvious this had not occurred to him. He looked around at his companions, who refused to meet his eyes as they hung their heads in shame. He took a deep breath and shook his head.

"Fool," roared Zarku. "You should have killed the dogs before leaving. Pinjaur's Panchayat will have more dogs and guards tomorrow night. How difficult is it to capture one villager at a time and make him one of us? Could you not get one single person from anywhere? Kalka? Saha? Sadhupur?"

Jeevan writhed on the ground in misery. The rest of his people stood behind him in absolute silence, not daring to look up. A cold smile spread across Zarku's face as he caressed his own bald head lovingly.

"You have failed me," he said in a soft voice laden with menace. "And so, you must be punished."

Jeevan stood up and edged backward.

"How sad that you are called Jeevan, meaning 'Life.' Your name is about to change to Mrityu ... 'Death.'"

Zarku's eye pulsed ominously, red light seeping out from the edges. The eyelid opened a tiny bit at a time and a red-hot ray bathed Jeevan, a pinpoint at first and then steadily growing into a powerful beam.

Jeevan grunted and sobbed, trying to edge away from the scorching red beam that grew in intensity with every passing second. Ugly red blisters pockmarked his body and became larger as one ran into the other and his skin melted into a river of green slime. His hair and flesh sizzled, giving off the most nauseating smell of rotten eggs and feces. His heart swelled and burst within his chest. Zarku's third eye was now fully open and the leader of the Vetalas was ablaze. He howled in agony and, within seconds, crumbled into a mound of ash. The rest of the Vetalas looked aghast.

"You," Zarku said, pointing to another large Vetala. "Come here."

The large man shuffled forward, not daring to look Zarku in the eye.

"You will now lead the rest. Tomorrow you will come to Morni. Meet me near the old well at midnight and I will tell you which men I want captured. They are the strong ones, likely to oppose me. Once they are gone, the weak ones can be overpowered in one night! Fail me and you will join your friend here," said Zarku, his eyes resting upon the heap of ashes.

"GO!" he called out as he strode away and disappeared into the darkness.

Tara's face was wet with tears.

"Suraj, they've gone."

Suraj, who had refused to look at the gruesome scene, lifted his head from Tara's shoulder. His face was streaked with tears, too.

"Time's running out, Didi, isn't it?"

CHAPTER 8
A LONG AND TERRIBLE NIGHT

"CRACK!" A huge sound reverberated overhead as if the sky had broken into two.

Oh no, thought Tara. *It's going to rain and we have no shelter.*

The sound of thunder rolled across the sky and jagged lightning stretched from one end of the horizon to the other. A soft pattering started and a cool wind swept through the trees. A few drops of cold rain touched their faces. Tara shivered. Without further warning, the skies opened and needles of rain came hurtling down, drenching everything with an equal mercilessness.

Within seconds, Tara and Suraj were soaked. The rain had come so suddenly that they had had no time to pull out the reed mats from their bundles. Their icy clothes clung to their wet skin as they pressed closer to each other, huddled under the tree. It afforded very little shelter and the rain continued unabated. Tara tugged at the bundle she carried but she was shivering so much that she could barely undo the knot. She gave up and moved closer to Suraj. After a few hours that seemed like an eternity to them, the deluge stopped. It was pitch black. Water dripped steadily onto the forest floor. The sounds of the night prowlers came back in full force.

Cold and shivering, they waited for daylight. The forest was alive around them, roaring, hooting, slithering, and howling. They jumped each time the noise came too close. Occasionally, Tara heard the squeal or yelp of a helpless animal uttering its last cry. She wondered how long it would be before it was their turn. She chanted every prayer she knew, to every deity they had ever worshipped, with a special prayer to Lord Ganesh.

"Didi, please can we light a fire now?"

"No Suraj, there are too many wild animals around. We cannot risk it."

"But I'm s-soo cold," he stuttered, his teeth chattering.

Tara cuddled him and massaged his thin body energetically. Cold, wet, and exhausted, they finally fell asleep.

● ● ●

When Tara awoke, it was noon. The sun was directly overhead and it caressed her with warm fingers of golden light from between the treetops, driving away the chill in the air. Suraj was nowhere in sight. Tara looked around, her heart hammering.

"Suraj," she croaked. Then louder, "Suraj, where are you?"

A tuft of black hair peeked out from a sal tree directly in front of her, followed by twinkling eyes and an impish grin.

"Good morning, Didi. I was searching for some dry wood to start a fire. Let's eat, I'm sooooo hungry."

When she saw him, Tara let out a deep breath. They had both survived the first night in the forest. She stood up and stretched her stiff limbs. She undid one of the bundles and pulled out a small steel vessel. Suraj had already arranged three flattish rocks for a makeshift fireplace. Tara poured enough water to make tea. Using one of the matches, she lit a small fire with the dry twigs Suraj had gathered. She huddled close to the fire so that her damp clothes could dry out. Suraj hugged his knees, staring into space.

"Didi, about last night ..."

Tara shot him a sharp look.

"Zarku is the one turning the villagers into Vetalas. He's the one pretending to cure them, too."

"Yes," said Tara.

"Shouldn't we go back and warn Rakaji?"

Tara continued making the tea, turning the question over in her mind.

"Grandfather is our only hope. We have to find him — fast!"

"Where will we find him, Didi? The forest is so big."

"We'll start at the Devi Temple. He meditated there years ago."

The water started boiling. Tara poured some milk and added four teaspoons of sugar. The brown liquid bubbled up to the top of the vessel like a small volcano spewing brown lava. She lifted it off the fire using the edge of her shawl and placed it on the ground to cool. She took a few chappatis from the bundle and flipped them on to the warm rocks. Within seconds they were toasty brown. She called Suraj and they sat down cross-legged near the warm fire to enjoy their simple breakfast. The vessel had cooled sufficiently and they took turns dipping the chappatis into the tea and sipping it straight from the vessel. Around them, sunlight swirled and danced as a light wind rustled the treetops. An occasional leaf drifted loose and spiralled lazily to the forest floor. Tara revelled in the serenity and freedom, free from constant abuse, free from painful taunts, and free from the endless housework. She could not remember when last she had enjoyed a meal in such peace.

She took a deep breath and closed her eyes. A distant growl reminded her that she did not have all day to dream. She jumped up and started packing.

"We have to find shelter today, Suraj. We were lucky last night. We may not be as lucky again."

Suraj nodded. He was enjoying his freedom, too. He ran from one shrub to another, examining the colourful flowers that had sprouted in the aftermath of the rain. He jumped up to catch a yellow and black butterfly. A burst of red, yellow, and green sailed from one tree to another.

"Parrots," said Suraj, pointing.

"Come *on*, Suraj, we have no time to waste."

They walked with a spring in their step, energized by the breakfast and the cool morning, and headed north toward the purple smudge of hills in the distance.

The land was gradually sloping upwards. A few hours passed as they traipsed on. They saw monkeys, deer, a few squirrels, and a couple of brown hares along the way, but no shelter. Suraj was starting to lag behind.

"Hurry up, Suraj. Why are you so slow?"

"I'm so tired, Didi, and I feel funny."

Tara frowned as she came up to him and touched his forehead. He seemed warm. Could it be the exertion of carrying the heavy bundle?

"Let's rest for a short while."

They chanced upon a small, cold stream that bubbled through the thick foliage. Tara would never have discovered it if she had not stepped into it and felt the cold water trickle into her shoe. Both knelt, scooped the water into their cupped hands, and let it trickle down their parched throats. Tara filled up their animal skin with the water and then bathed Suraj's warm forehead and face. He was looking flushed and her heart thudded with anxiety. They had started late in the day and evening was already upon them. If they did not find a place to shelter soon ...

Suraj dragged his feet for the next couple of hours as

Tara peered at every crevasse and crack with hopeful eyes. Once again, night threw her black cloak around them and the light went out like a snuffed candle. The night chorus started.

Suraj was sagging against Tara now and she was very worried. She put a hand to his forehead. He was burning with fever.

Oh no, not now. Not when we are so exposed, thought Tara in despair. She would have to get Suraj comfortable and bring his fever down. She headed for the nearest tree and sat Suraj down. She dug into her bundle and groped for matches. She knew the fire would attract animals, but she had to boil herbs for medicine to bring down Suraj's fever. Tara said a fervent prayer as she undid the bundle of dry twigs they had gathered earlier that morning and struck the match to give her some light. A distance away from the tree she put down a few twigs and threw the lit match on them. They caught fire immediately and within a few minutes she had a strong fire going.

"Suraj," she whispered. "Suraj, talk to me."

He mumbled incoherently under his breath. Tara laid him down on his warm bedding and covered him with a blanket. She propped his head up and poured some water into his mouth. He was unable to swallow and the water trickled out the side. With growing apprehension, Tara realized that he was very sick.

"Please Lord Ganesh, make him well again. I need him. I can't do this alone. I just *can't*!"

Tears slid down her cheeks as she cradled Suraj's head and prayed. Suraj moaned in his sleep. *I have to try and get some medicine into him*, Tara thought.

She reached for the small bag of herbs and undid the knot with shaking fingers. In it were a few pale yellow fruits: dried amla and dried fronds of the tulsi plant. She took one of each and carefully wrapped up the bundle of precious medicinal herbs and put them away. Tara put on some water to boil, dropped the amla and tulsi into it, and watched as the mixture turned a yellowish brown.

Suraj tossed and turned, muttering nonsensical things. Tara darted anxious looks in his direction.

"Let me go ... Mother where are you?" Suraj muttered. "I'm coming, wait for me."

Tara took the vessel off the fire with shaking hands. Her mother had taught her that the forest had all that one ever needed: food, medicine, and shelter. Tara had often watched her make complicated medicines from common plants and herbs to cure the villagers. The tulsi and amla plants were well known for their therapeutic effects on fevers and colds. She was thankful that she had had the presence of mind to pack them.

Darkness lapped at the edges of the fire. She looked around uneasily as she waited for the water to cool. Now and then she saw movement: glinting red and yellow eyes. Nothing came close and she was relieved. She could not have warded off the attack of a wild beast just then. She tested the water with her forefinger. It was lukewarm. She took it to where Suraj lay and, cradling his head in her lap, tilted the vessel so that the liquid trickled into his mouth.

Suraj gagged, spluttered, and sat up weakly as the water shot straight out of his mouth. He fell back on the bed, breathing heavily.

"You have to drink this, Suraj. Come on, please try," pleaded Tara.

She wiped his mouth with the edge of her shawl and tried again. Once again, Suraj coughed and spluttered, but not a drop of medicine went down his throat. Finally, she took the edge of her shawl and dipped it into the water. She gently squeezed the drops into Suraj's mouth and waited till he swallowed. Painstakingly, she fed him the medicine, drop by drop, till half the liquid was in him. Suraj was breathing peacefully, now in a deep sleep. She moved a strand of hair from his damp forehead and, leaning forward, kissed him. She sat with her back to the trunk, ready for a night-long vigil. Distant roaring and snarling kept her from dozing off.

She stared into the fire, watching the flames reaching up to the night sky, occasional sparks swallowed by the darkness.

"I should never have left home. I am responsible if he dies."

"Didi," said Suraj in a faint voice.

"Yes, Suraj," she said, crawling to where he lay.

"Didi, I'm so tired. I want to sleep forever and ever."

"WHAT?" she said, fear clutching her heart. She shook

him gently. "Suraj, don't say that. You'll get well soon. You must. Talk to me ... SURAJ!"

She cradled his head in her hands and gazed intently at the flushed face. His eyes were already closed and even as she uttered the words, a sense of foreboding gripped her. She lay down next to Suraj and hugged his burning body to hers as tears streamed down her cheeks unchecked.

"Don't leave me, little brother. Please don't leave me."

• • •

The long night marched steadily toward dawn. Several times she saw gleaming yellow eyes in the gloom around her. The small golden-orange fire bobbed like a boat of light, adrift on a turbulent sea of darkness. A light fog sent wispy fingers curling around them so that Tara seemed to be looking through a gauze veil.

She sat up and occasionally walked around to keep awake, but as dawn approached, the urge to sleep was so overpowering that she closed her eyes, telling herself it was only for a short while. The last thing she saw as her eyelids drooped was Suraj. His forehead had turned a silvery black. His eyes had disappeared. How could that be? She forced her eyelids to open. A black band on his head? And it was moving? It was the last thing she remembered before she fell into a deep sleep.

Chapter 9
A Brother is Lost and Found

When Tara awoke, all was still. Pale light filtered through a swaying green roof and it took her a moment to realize she was in the forest. The angle of the sun was all wrong. It should have been overhead, but instead it came from somewhere to the side.

The setting sun.

It was evening.

She had slept the day away.

She was tired and aching all over. Why was she so tired and why had she slept all day ...?

"SURAJ!" she screamed as everything came flooding back.

HE WAS GONE!

The bedding on which he had lain next to her was empty.

She was all alone.

"SURAJ!" she screamed again as she jumped up and

ran, panic-stricken, first in one direction and then the other.

Silence.

"Please, Suraj, don't play games. Be a good boy and come out."

Silence.

No, he couldn't be gone. He was playing hide and seek again. But he was too ill and weak. That meant ...

"Noooooo!" she moaned.

She envisioned a wild animal dragging him away as he lay unconscious. And she had slept through all of it. She had let him die. *It was all her fault.* She rocked back and forth, sobbing loudly, her chest heaving as grief poured out of her in waves. How could she have been so careless? She was responsible for the death of her brother.

"Why, Lord Ganesh, why him? Why my brother?" she sobbed. "Why did you let this happen?"

Tara covered her face and sank to the ground, devastated. For hours she sobbed, oblivious of the waning day, the mosquitoes, and that she had not eaten anything. Finally, her tears were spent. She felt so alone and empty. It seemed as if her own shadow had deserted her.

She sat on Suraj's bedding and clutched his blanket. She inhaled its fragrance: that particularly sweet, sweaty smell that she knew so well. Wrapping herself in it she let the memories of Suraj wash over her.

Tara did not know how long she sat staring as the sun slipped below the lip of the horizon. She had no recollection of the day turning to night. All she could think of was the previous night, when Suraj lay burning with fever while she kept vigil. Now he was gone, leaving behind nothing but a bittersweet fragrance. She wrapped the blanket tighter around her and lay back staring at the stars, which winked at her, as if laughing at some private joke.

"I want him back. I want my brother back," she said over and over again. She knew it would not help. If only she had not fallen asleep last night. If only ... but it was too late for regrets. Maybe if she made a bonfire, wild animals would be attracted to her and then ... and then she'd be with him sooner.

Tara dragged herself up wearily. She groped her way to the bundles, dug out a candle, and lit it. She pushed it into the soil in the lee of a rock and searched for firewood. In the light of the flickering candle Tara gathered as much wood as she could and piled it on top of the ashes of last night's fire. There was no wind and the candle burned straight and tall, throwing her gigantic shadow on the trees behind her. Once she had a big enough pile, she stepped back to survey it. This would burn through the night. Who knows, if she was lucky, she might not have long to wait.

As if on cue, a growl sounded in the distance and was followed by a long, low howl. Not long now.

She plucked up the candle to light the bonfire when a totally unexpected sound reached her. Tara froze, straining to hear the sound. There was silence. *My imagination is running wild*, she thought.

Tara had just bent to light the wood when a faint breeze stirred the leaves, bringing the same sound — again. Her hand shook and hot wax dripped onto it. She yelped and dropped the candle, which went out. She was in near-complete darkness. A sliver of moon peeped from the edge of a cloud. Who was sobbing in the middle of the forest? Tara did not relight the candle. She stood still and heard the sobbing start again. She walked toward it.

Don't go, said the small voice inside her. *Don't go*. But she kept walking. The sound was reeling her in, like a fish on a line. The faint light of the silvery moon barely lit the way but she was following her ears and her heart ... *her heart*? She was surprised that the sound of sobbing could move her so much. She walked deeper and deeper into the jungle and the voice grew louder.

"Mother, I miss you so much," said a male voice, and Tara's heart skipped a beat.

That voice. She'd heard it before, but never like this. She crept forward. A dark shape loomed directly ahead. Tara stuffed her knuckle in her mouth to stop from screaming. As her eyes adjusted to the gloom, she saw that the shape had not moved. She reached out a trembling hand. Her fingertips brushed a rough surface. She pressed her palms against it: cool stone. Her panic subsided a bit as she went on. Her heart ached and tears pricked her eyelids. The sound of sobbing had died away but she felt like crying, too.

What was it about this place? It was some kind of building, or temple. Suddenly she remembered that Parvati used to speak about an abandoned temple in the heart of the forest. Long ago it was used frequently. But something had happened that had caused the villagers to remove the deities of the holy trinity — lords Brahma, Vishnu, and Shiva — move them to another location, and abandon this temple. The path to it was overgrown and most had even forgotten it existed.

Tara moved forward cautiously as thorny shrubs tore at her blanket. She rounded the corner, gasped, and ducked behind the temple wall. Her heart was hammering so loudly that she thought he would definitely hear it and come running at her.

She took a few deep breaths and the roaring in her ears lessened. She peered round the corner once again. Sitting on the stone steps was Zarku. He had his head in his hands and was sobbing uncontrollably. Tara shook her head. She closed her eyes and popped them open again, hoping the vision would disappear. But no, there he was. Except that Zarku was not sobbing anymore. He was holding up a silver thread, which glinted in the moonlight. Zarku held it up and watched it sway in the breeze. Suddenly, he made a fist and the silver thread disappeared into its depth.

"Mother, if you could see me now, you would be so proud of me. I am Zarku ... the best healer in all of India ... and I made it, all on my own."

Zarku opened his palm and the silver thread glistened.

Tara strained to hear what Zarku was saying in a low voice. Maybe if she found out something about him, a weakness, she would be able to help Prabala defeat him.

"When you died, Mother," continued Zarku, "you left me with Father, who blamed me for your death. He HATED me. Hated me so much that he wished I would die too. He told me so. The only thing he gave me freely and with love were curses and beatings."

Zarku's voice was hoarse as he said it and Tara felt tears pricking her eyelids. She was feeling sorry for this monster?

"And what did you give me, Mother? An ugly outgrowth on my forehead that people thought was another eye. Everyone teased me about it and beat me up over it."

Zarku stood up and paced the clearing in front of the temple. Hidden by the stone steps, Tara prayed that he would not sense her presence. She held her breath as he came within a few steps of her and strode away, still ranting.

"I was ready to join you, Mother, tired of the beatings and the jeering. I went to the old well to drown myself ... but then ...," Zarku giggled.

Tara cringed at the cruelty she heard in that soft giggle.

"Then I met him, my saviour, Kubera, the Lord of the Underworld. He promised me *revenge*. Revenge on all those who had mocked my deformity. He helped me, Mother. He turned my deformity into my greatest strength."

Zarku caressed his third eye.

"This, Mother, is the eye that can see into the heart

and mind. I can sense strength and weakness in people. And I can make then bow to my will."

Tara sank to the ground trembling as she continued to clutch the blanket tightly. Now she understood why Zarku was destroying the villagers. He had made a deal with the Lord of the Underworld to avenge himself. They were all doomed unless someone could stop him.

Zarku had stopped pacing and was standing in front of a wooden post directly in front of the temple. He hung the silver thread from a sliver of bark and ran his fingertips along it, still talking.

"Mother, I've missed you. If you'd been here, things might have been different. But there's no going back. I promised Kubera that in return for this gift, I would give him the souls of the undead. Once I had the villagers under my control, they would do my bidding and their souls would be Kubera's. Only if someone turned them back to their human form would they be free. But that's not going to happen, is it? Only one person can stop me: Prabala. And he'll be dead soon."

"NO!" yelled Tara.

Zarku's head snapped in her direction.

Tara was aghast. She had not realized that she had yelled out and stood up at the same time.

Suddenly, she was staring into the deep, dark pools of Zarku's eyes.

"Well, well, well, what have we here? Tara, isn't it?"

Tara stared at him. How did he know her name?

"Yes, I know your name. And who your grandfather is, though he won't be around for long," said Zarku as he grabbed Tara and dragged her to the wooden post, flinging her against it.

The back of Tara's head cracked with such force that she saw stars. She barely felt something cool slip past her cheek.

"You little busybody. Thought you could hear my secrets and tell everyone?" snarled Zarku.

The sobbing little boy was gone. In his place stood Zarku, the monster who only lived for revenge. Tara stared at him, unable to speak. His third eye started to open. She cringed and hugged the post for support, waiting for the searing heat that would turn her to a mound of ash.

Nothing happened.

She turned to look at Zarku, who was staring at her with those whiteless eyes.

"My third eye won't open," he breathed. "I DON'T UNDERSTAND THIS!"

Tara released a deep and shaky breath.

For a moment, they stood staring at each other in the silent moonlit clearing. Tara stood frozen while Zarku studied her with his eyes narrowed. Suddenly, she turned and ran. Zarku did not follow.

As she disappeared behind the temple, she heard him call out.

"My Vetalas will find you, Tara, and they will complete the job I was not able to do. Watch your back."

● ● ●

It was more luck than anything that guided Tara back to where she had left her things. She felt as if she was in some kind of weird dream and unable to make sense of anything. Tara stumbled to the bedding, lay down, and fell into an exhausted sleep.

She awoke once more to the cacophony of bird calls and sunlight glinting through an undulating green ceiling. And she was still alive. She sat up and clasped her knees to her chest, deep in thought. The sun was still shining, the birds still singing. She had been through so much in the last day and night. She had lost her beloved brother and then discovered Zarku's past. What was more shocking was that he had been unable to kill her. *I wonder why?* she asked herself.

Tara stood up and shook out Suraj's blanket to put it away. Something dropped out of the folds and sparkled in the morning sunlight. Tara bent to retrieve it. It was the silver thread Zarku had been talking to last night: an anklet. It was heavy and the beaten silver was in an intricate design. It must have been his mother's and when it had fallen into her blanket, it had protected her. That seemed to be the only reason she was still alive. Tara said a prayer to his mother, slipped the bracelet into the bundle, and finished packing.

She sat down to think. It was now more important than ever to find Prabala before Zarku and the Vetalas did.

But could she do it alone? Suraj and she had set out on this journey believing that their mother and grandfather were alive. She *would* carry on alone and find them. Suraj's death would not be in vain.

Tara headed north. She gathered edible roots and berries to munch. The food she had packed was long gone but she still had a bit of water left. She would manage till she reached a village.

Tara was deep in thought as she continued walking. She hated doing anything alone, always seeking out Suraj's companionship. Now she had no choice. And she found that she was not as scared as she thought she might be. A small frisson of pride shot through her. *I can do this*, she thought. She marched on, keeping a sharp eye on the moss-covered forest floor. Then she saw it: a small path made by bare feet. She hurried along it. The trees started thinning around her and sunlight poured through in large patches of liquid gold.

All of a sudden she stopped. She heard a faint chant in the distance. The voices came closer ... still closer ... and her heart started thumping. She stepped off the path and cautiously dodged from tree to tree. Had Zarku sent his Vetalas? But she knew they only came out at night. Had her wicked stepmother sent a search party to haul them back home? It couldn't be; she was miles away from Morni. Was her father searching for them? Not possible — he did not care about them at all.

Who could it be?

"Ram Nam Satya Hai."

"Ram Nam Satya Hai."

The chant for the dead. Now she understood, and her heart slowed its frantic beat. A group of villagers were carrying one of their dead to the burning ground outside the village. She had never seen a funeral pyre and she was curious. Children were normally not allowed to watch a Sati ceremony, though she had heard about it in the stories that their father had told them. Most of the villagers believed that cremation purified the soul of the dead. The ashes were then scattered by the eldest son of the family into the holy Ganges River so that the soul would be one with the Gods.

As the voices drew nearer she hid behind the trunk of a large tree. The procession passed her by and she saw four men holding the legs of a cot, on which lay a body covered in white cotton from head to toe. Many men followed the cot and its bearers, calling out the chant of the dead. A lone woman followed, dressed in a dazzling white saree. Her long, black hair framed a pale face. She seemed to be completely oblivious of her surrounding and was half dragged, half carried by two villagers.

Tara squeezed her eyes shut. The woman was the widow of the dead man and was being forced to perform Sati." Her blood ran cold and she clamped her hand to her mouth to prevent herself from crying out to stop them. Sati was the destiny of any girl or woman who had the misfortune to become a widow. It was an age-old tradition where the woman was forced to burn herself on her husband's funeral pyre. It was such a terrifying ordeal that most women (and sometimes mere girls) had to be drugged into submission so that they did not rebel, or so that they wouldn't realize what was happening till it was too late. Tara shivered, despite the warmth of the afternoon sun.

She turned back to look at the procession, which was moving away rapidly. Suddenly, she noticed a tall, thin boy trailing behind, desperately trying to push through the men to get to the woman. He seemed to be twelve or thirteen, slightly older than Tara. He wore a muddied white kurta and his pyjamas were torn at the knee. *She must be his mother*, Tara thought. And it was evident he was trying to prevent her from committing Sati.

"Mother, wake up! MOTHER, it's me, your son Ananth. Please, Mother, look at me," he sobbed in a hoarse voice.

"Go away," growled a ferocious-looking villager. "This is your mother's destiny. No one can change it and it's no use throwing a tantrum. Now behave, or you will incur the wrath of Lord Yama."

He shoved Ananth hard, and Ananth fell to the side of the road, struck his head against a rock, and lay there dazed. The procession sped on and disappeared round a bend.

The boy sat up, hugged his knees, and sobbed quietly. Tara dropped the bundles and ran to him, wondering what to say. She had never seen a boy his age cry and was unsure of how to deal with it. Finally, she sat next to him and patted his shoulder.

For a few moments, the boy was completely unaware of Tara. After a while, his sobs subsided. He looked up and noticed Tara. Brown eyes looked into black ones.

"I've lost my father and my mother," said Ananth without any preamble.

"I know," said Tara, squeezing his shoulder.

Ananth started sobbing again, soft low sobs that seemed to rise unbidden from deep within him.

"Get her back. Please, save her," he wept.

Tears welled up in Tara's eyes and cascaded down her cheeks. She wiped them away. She left the bundles near Ananth and raced after the funeral procession. Maybe she could squeeze through the crowd and grab his mother just before the men set her on fire. She did not even know how they went about it, but she had to try.

"Aaaaargh," someone yelled out from the head of the procession.

Everyone came to an abrupt halt. Tara froze. She peeped out cautiously from behind a tree and turned icy cold at the sight. A huge tiger crouched in front of the procession. Saliva dripped from his bared fangs and his tail flicked from side to side in agitation.

The men holding the cot threw it down so quickly that the body almost rolled off. They scattered into the jungle like shards of a smashed pot, one villager passing so close to Tara that she felt his warm breath on her skin. Within seconds, the road was empty except for the widow and her dead husband. The woman stood in a trance, unaware of the danger that faced her.

The tiger advanced toward her with a menacing growl. The chilly air and the growls of the tiger finally penetrated the widow's stupor. Tara saw her eyes widen in shock as she shuffled backward and collided with her husband's cot. She sat down at the head of his body, quivering. Tara was unable to move. Horrified, she continued to watch.

The tiger took one step forward and then another. Tara could see every whisker on its face; all its yellowed teeth were bared as it advanced on Ananth's mother, and then it roared. The widow screamed in terror and fell back on the cot.

Tara could not watch anymore. She ran back to Ananth, trying to wipe out the image of the tiger and his mother.

Coward, a voice inside her said.

But what could I have done? she argued back. *Give the tiger another juicy tidbit?*

I can't tell Ananth about this, she thought. *He has enough to deal with already.*

She reached Ananth, panting hard. He looked up at her, a question in his moist eyes.

Tara shook her head.

"I could not catch up. They were too far ahead."

Ananth's head sank back onto his chest.

Tara reached out, took his hand in hers, and gently tugged it. She helped him to his feet and led him to where the bundles lay. Once she was sure he was steady on his feet, she stooped to pick up the bundles.

"I've lost someone too," she said. "My brother. I know what it feels like."

Ananth shuffled quietly beside her. There was a deep silence.

"My name is Tara. You're Ananth aren't you? I heard you call out your name. I'm from Morni. And you are from ...?"

"Ropar," answered Ananth in a husky voice. "We were so happy," he continued. "Then Father died and our world fell apart. I lost a father and now I'm going to lose my mother. It's so unfair."

His grief overwhelmed him again and his feet crumpled under him. He sat down and covered his face as if ashamed to be so out of control. Tara sat quietly beside him, remembering yesterday.

After a while, Tara stood up and paced, shooting glances at Ananth. Spending the night in the open was making her jittery again. Wasn't he ever going to stop crying? She had to do something.

"Ananth, you have to help me. We need to find shelter. The forest is too dangerous." Her eyes glistened with tears and her voice trembled. Ananth sat there staring into space.

"Ananth, GET UP," she said, shaking his shoulder. "We can't sit here. We have to move, NOW! Let's go back to Ropar."

"NO!" he yelled.

"Why not?" asked Tara

"I-I can't go back. There's nothing there but memories. Where are you going?"

"To find my mother and grandfather."

"Why?" said Ananth

"I'll tell you later. Can we start walking?" asked Tara, an edge to her voice.

"Where to?"

"Do you know a safe place to spend the night?"

"Yes," Ananth said after a moment's silence. "It's a bit of a climb into the mountains. There are some hidden caves where my friends and I used to play. Let's go."

He stood up and held out his hand for one of the bundles. Tara handed it over gratefully. Her back was sore with the extra weight. They started walking away from the village and the path that the procession had taken. Ananth took a last look in the direction that his mother had disappeared. He stared at the brown smudges in the mud almost as if he could see the footprints of his mother's small feet. He stooped and picked up a handful of mud and let it trickle slowly through his hand.

Tara stood silently, an ache in her heart. She had not even had the chance to say goodbye to Suraj.

Abruptly, Ananth stood up and started walking. Tara followed.

• • •

"How did your father die?" asked Tara.

Ananth marched silently. Now and then a tear trickled down his cheek. His pace did not slacken and Tara matched his stride in spite of the stitch in her side.

"There is something very evil in the forest," said Ananth. "Men from our village have been disappearing. No one wants to go into the forests now. Food and firewood are becoming scarce."

"It's happening in Morni, too," replied Tara in a listless voice.

"So, what happened to your father?" she asked again.

"He was hunting hares in the forest. He came back late one night. We could barely recognize him; there was a deep gash on his forehead," said Ananth taking a deep breath to steady his voice.

"And his skin was a translucent green and his feet were at an awkward angle?" finished Tara.

"How did you know that?"

"The same happened to a boy named Ravi in Morni," replied Tara.

"A man who called himself one of the best healers in these parts appeared and took my father to his hut. That was the last time we saw Father alive," said Ananth, his chest heaving with anger and sorrow. "My mother wanted to go with him, but the healer refused her. He said no one could see him healing the sick or it would not work.

Father died and we were given his body back to perform the last rites.

"I'll never forget his evil face: that shark-like smile, that bald head, the black robe. He called himself —"

"— Zarku," said Tara and Ananth simultaneously

"You know him?" asked Ananth.

"Yes. He took the place of my grandfather, Prabala, who used to be the village healer. Since he came, many men have disappeared, especially the ones that openly challenge his skills. The ones that have accepted him are unharmed," said Tara. "I think he only preys on the strong ones likely to stand up to him. Did your father oppose Zarku in any way? Question his authority?"

"Yes," said Ananth bitterly. "He tried to tell the Panchayat that Zarku was evil. Soon after, he died. You think the disappearances are related to Zarku?"

"I am sure of it. I saw him last night."

Ananth stopped and Tara walked straight into him.

"What? You saw Zarku?"

Tara nodded, and quickly recounted everything she had seen and heard.

"I felt sorry for him when he was sobbing," she said "He missed his mother just like you and I do."

"Are you mad, Tara?"

"What do you mean?" asked Tara in a cold voice.

"You're sorry for a monster that kills people?"

Tara shrugged.

"Zarku's father blamed him for his mother's death

and beat him often," said Tara. "Many others made fun of the deformity on his forehead. That is why he wants revenge ..."

"You think I care?" said Ananth, his face red, his chest heaving. "He should be captured, tortured, and killed."

"So how does that make you different from Zarku?" shot back Tara, equally angry.

"Oh shut up!" said Ananth. "Girls don't know anything!"

The air shimmered with a tinge of red as Tara faced him, her hands on her hips.

"Don't you dare say that to me again! You think you know more because you're a *boy*? HA!" said Tara, her eyes flashing ominously.

"Let's not get into this now," said Ananth. "So his mother's anklet protects you?"

"It did last night. But I don't know how long it will work. That's another reason we have to find shelter. He is going to send the Vetalas after me," said Tara in a shrill voice.

"Don't worry," said Ananth, pointing. "It's not too far now. We must find your grandfather. Prabala is well known in my village. He is said to be the best healer in all of India. He is probably the only one who can stop this monster. Do you know where to look for him, Tara?"

"The Devi Temple in the Shivalik Range that separates the two lakes. It was the place where Grandfather often went to meditate. It is definitely a place to start."

"I'd like to help, Tara. I've become an orphan, but at least I can prevent my fate befalling other children," said Ananth, his mouth a thin line.

"That's what my brother and I set out to do," said Tara, her face clouding.

"And that is exactly what we are going to do, Tara. I just hope we are not too late."

CHAPTER 10
FLASHBACK

Tara's breath came in gasps. The exertion of climbing the steep mountain trail with a heavy bundle was taking its toll on her.

Ananth climbed steadily, reaching out now and then to pull Tara over a rough patch. The narrow path snaked around the mountain and as the light faded, the climb became more treacherous. A bone-chilling breeze swept down the mountainside and straight into their unprotected faces. They shook with cold and exhaustion.

"How much longer, Ananth? I can-n-not-t walk anym-more," said Tara through frozen lips.

"Just a little bit further, Tara. We're almost there."

Tara willed her mind to forget the pain raging through her exhausted body and kept going.

All of a sudden, Ananth shrugged off his bundle and jumped onto something.

"What is that?" asked Tara

"Dinner!" said Ananth, holding up something long that wriggled furiously. He swept his hand in an arc and dashed a hare onto the ground. It gave a small whimper and was silent. Tara gasped.

"Did you have to do that?" she asked in a pained voice. "We could have fruits or berries."

"Do you see any fruits around?" asked Ananth.

Tara shook her head.

"Any berries?"

Tara shook her head again.

"Feel like eating grass?"

Tara made a face.

"We have to eat to keep our strength up," said Ananth. "Packed any spices or salt?"

Tara nodded. "I've got some tandoori masala, and salt, too."

"Good," said Ananth. "At least we won't have to eat it plain. Here we are," he said as soon as a large rock, like an inverted V, came into view.

With their goal so near, an extra burst of energy seemed to infuse their limbs. They scrambled up the last few feet and reached a curtain of vines. It lay like a still, green veil on the face of the mountain. Ananth went up to the green curtain and, thrusting his hand through it, pulled it aside to reveal a large, black cavern.

"Throw the bundles into the cave, Tara, and help me collect some firewood."

Tara chucked their bundles into the gaping darkness and turned to help Ananth. They collected armloads of dry wood and piled them up at the mouth of the cave. Finally, cold and exhausted, they crawled inside and lay down on the dirt floor to catch their breath. Ananth was the first to get up.

"We have to eat, Tara. Get up and help me cook the hare."

He stepped out and brought in an armload of wood. The cave floor was dry. The light of the moon filtered in through the fronds, casting a silvery light into the dim depths. He found a couple of rocks at the entrance of the cave, which he positioned a few feet apart to roast the hare.

"Tara, do you have a knife, matches? Come *on*, don't just lie there, help me!"

Tara gave a deep sigh, pulled a bundle to her, dug out the matches, knife, and packets of masala and salt, and threw them to him. It felt so good to be looked after for a change. In a few moments, Ananth had a fire going. He sat on his haunches and held his palms out to the flames. Tara rolled onto her side and looked into the flames as they reached out with wispy orange fingers to touch the low ceiling. The cave was perfect. It was small, cosy, and warming up nicely. As Ananth busied himself stacking the bundles neatly in a corner and laying out the bedding so that they did not have to sit on the hard floor, Tara gazed into the fire.

"If only we had found this two nights ago, Suraj would still be with me."

Her voice quavered.

"Suraj is your brother?" asked Ananth, without turning around.

"My younger brother," said Tara. "He had a high fever. I tried to stay awake but could not. When I woke up he was gone. I think wild animals ..."

She burst into tears at the realization that just a few hours ago his small living body had been close to her. Now she would never get to hug him, look into his laughing face, hear him say "Didi" in a hundred different tones depending on his mood.

"Tara, don't think of the past. It hurts too much. I'll be your brother now. I'll look after you. I promise," said Ananth, coming up to her and stroking her hair.

"Really?" asked Tara, gazing at him with a tear-streaked face. "You promise you won't leave me?"

Ananth pulled a loose thread from his kurta and handed it to her, holding out his right hand. "Go on. We don't have a rakhi, but this thread will do just fine."

Tara took the thread and, with shaking hands, tied the flimsy cotton thread to Ananth's wrist, completing an age-old ceremony of love between brother and sister. Then he went back to preparing the meal.

"So, why did you run away?" he asked as he began skinning and cleaning the hare near the mouth of the cave.

Tara sighed deeply. "To find my mother and my grandfather."

"And you say they'll be at the Devi Temple?"

Tara shrugged.

"That's what I need to find out. I know he is still alive."

"We will find him," said Ananth. "We need him back."

Ananth washed the hare with the water out of the animal skin and took it to the fire. He smeared the hare with the red tandoori masala mixed with salt, then skewered it from head to tail using a stout branch and laid it on the rocks.

"And your mother?" asked Ananth.

"She was special, too."

"How so?"

"She could see into the future," said Tara.

"Really?" said Ananth, sitting back on his haunches and gaping at her. "What did she see?"

"Many things, but not all of it was good."

"Oh! Is that why ...," asked Ananth, and his voice trailed away.

"Can we not talk about it right now?" snapped Tara. "Please?" she said, noting the hurt expression on Ananth's face. "Since she left, our life has turned upside down."

"Sorry," said Ananth, staring into the flames. "But if you get it off your chest, you may feel better."

A wonderful fragrance of roast hare was starting to fill the cave. Occasionally, the fire hissed and crackled as a globule of fat from the meat dropped into the red-hot embers.

"As soon as Mother and Grandfather disappeared,

Father remarried Kali. I'm sure Zarku had something to do with Father remarrying even though we did not see him before Diwali night. Father allowed her to ill-treat us without a word in our defence. After I heard Kali plot with Zarku to kill us, we had to escape. And then I lost Suraj, my baby brother who I was responsible for. I let him die. What an unlucky person I am. I lose the ones that I love the most. Watch out, Ananth, or you'll be next."

Tara buried her face in her hands and sobbed.

"That is enough, Tara. Not a single word more," said Ananth sternly. "What's happened with your mother and brother is not your fault. You did the best you could. Look at me. I have lost both my parents. Am I not unluckier than you?"

Tara reached out and held his hand tightly.

"I am so glad I have you, Ananth. It hurts so much to go on living without my family. I wish I could die so we could all be together. I feel as much an orphan as you do. But," she said, squeezing his hand, "I have you, my brother, and we'll be all right together."

"We'll talk tomorrow. Now, eat this delicious hare I've cooked. You can't let it go to waste."

Surprisingly, Tara found that she was hungry. She gnawed at the meat, feeling spent yet light-hearted. After a couple of bites, Tara stopped eating and sniffed.

"Ananth, is this meat fresh?"

"Of course, silly! You saw me kill it in front of you. Why do you ask?"

"Then why does it smell rotten?" asked Tara, sniffing it all over. "I hope it does not have some kind of bone disease."

A large shadow, then two, then three, fell across the wall of the cave. Tara and Ananth both looked up in horror.

Tara screamed.

CHAPTER 11
THE VETALAS

Three large men with translucent green skin stood blocking the entrance. A foul smell emanating from them permeated every corner of the cave, making Tara nauseous. The men bared their broken, yellow teeth and grunted.

The Vetalas, thought Tara. *He's sent them to kill us.*

"What do you want?" asked Tara in a shaky voice.

Up close, they were so ugly that it almost hurt to keep eye contact. Each of the men had a deep gash on his forehead. Their eyes were black, as if having seen some terrible sight, the whites had dissolved completely.

The men grunted and advanced, one large, backward-turned foot at a time. They converged on Tara and Ananth, blocking escape.

Ananth inched backward and grabbed a burning twig from the fire. He scooped it up and threw it into the face of the nearest Vetala. The man swept it aside without any effort and continued advancing.

"Listen to me," pleaded Tara. "We have not harmed you in any way. Please spare us."

No reaction. Grunting, the Vetalas advanced.

Ananth launched himself at the nearest Vetala and started clawing at his face, while Tara flung whatever she could at them: pots, rocks, shoes, burning twigs. One of the twigs landed on the clothes of the Vetala closest to her and he lit up like a torch. He rolled on the ground, screaming in agony. His companions ignored him. The burning Vetala grunted and shrieked so loudly that Tara's ears were ringing. The fire engulfed him rapidly, and within moments he was a charred lump of sickly smelling flesh.

That left two. Enraged, the remaining Vetalas lunged at Tara and Ananth.

"Ananth, help," croaked Tara as rough hands closed tightly around her throat.

But Ananth had his hands full trying to prevent the other Vetala from getting a grip around his own neck. Tara kicked weakly as the cave started to go black.

Suddenly, Ananth twisted out of the grip of the Vetala he had been grappling with and made a dash for the entrance of the cave, which was unguarded.

He's running away, thought Tara as she gasped for breath. *He's leaving me with these monsters.*

Panic hammered at her chest. She was all alone!

"Ananth!" she started to yell, but no sound came out as she fought for breath. The green monster followed Ananth outside. Someone yelled, there was scuffling, and then silence. A sweat-soaked Ananth came dashing back into the cave as Tara still struggled with her attacker.

With a running leap, Ananth jumped onto the Vetala's back, clawing at his eyes.

"Aaaargh," the Vetala yelled. It reached back and slashed at Ananth's exposed face with long and dirty fingernails.

"Tara, the fire," gasped Ananth, starting to tire as the Vetala bucked and jumped.

Tara reached for the largest burning log and dragged it out of the fire. The burning wood singed her palms, but she did not feel a thing. She dropped the wood onto the Vetala's feet as he struggled with Ananth. The stench of scorching flesh filled the cave. Howling, the Vetala ran for freedom. Ananth jumped off and the shrieking Vetala disappeared into the night.

For a moment, there was silence. Tara sat up and dragged herself toward Ananth, who was lying still. He was bleeding profusely from the numerous cuts and scrapes on his arms and face. There was a particularly deep and ugly scratch on his right check that looked very painful.

"Ananth, are you all right?"

"Water," he croaked.

Tara ran to get the animal skin and brought it to him. She poured the cool water into his mouth, trying not to look too horrified at the bruises and cuts he had suffered. Revived, Ananth managed to crawl over to the bedding and collapsed on it. Tara built up the fire, all the while darting anxious looks at Ananth. She was lucky to have escaped with nothing more than a few scratches. Ananth had saved her. She dipped a cloth in water and started cleaning Ananth's wounds. Guilt coursed through her veins when she realized that he had saved her life and she had thought he was going to abandon her. *What a suspicious fool I am*, she chided herself bitterly as her hands moved gently across Ananth's face.

"Owww, ouch," came a steady stream from Ananth.

"Just a bit more, Ananth. Keep still."

He opened his eyes gradually.

"Tara, I'm hurting all over. It feels like I'm on fire. What if I ..."

"Shhh. Don't talk."

In a short while, she had cleaned up all his bruises as best as she could, though his face was starting to swell up and the cut on his cheek was an angry red, bursting at the seams.

"Not him too, Lord. You can't do this to me," she muttered.

As the night progressed, Ananth got worse. His skin was flushed and hot. A sudden fear gripped her as she realized that, once again, she was all alone, and it was up to her to save their lives and find her grandfather. The walls of the cave seemed to be closing in on her, squeezing all the air out. *Get a grip*, said a stern voice in her head. *You start panicking at the first sign of trouble. You don't have that luxury right now. Both your lives are in your hands.*

Yes, she thought. *I have to think clearly. Make some*

medicine to fight the poison, yes that's it. Tulsi, ritha, amla, and neem.

She realized with a sick feeling that she did not have any neem leaves. *Doesn't matter. Just make the best of what you have. Hurry ... you don't have time*, said the little voice.

With shaking hands she put the remaining water to boil and tipped the precious herbs into it. She kept checking on Ananth every few minutes. He was delirious.

"Ananth, talk to me. Say something," she begged as she blew on the infusion. Tears leaked out as she realized it had been a while since Ananth had last spoken. Some of her tears plopped into the cooling water. *I hope the salt does not ruin the medicine*, she thought, blowing hard to cool the concoction.

She ran to Ananth and, cradling his head in her lap, she tried to force his pale lips open to pour the liquid in. He did not respond at all, and she had to squeeze it into his mouth a few drops at a time. A sense of déjà vu came upon her as she prayed and cried alternately. The night was long. Ananth thrashed restlessly, the cut on his face becoming more livid and swollen, so that his cheek looked like a ripe fig about to burst.

In the quiet hours between night and dawn, Ananth stopped thrashing and Tara could feel the life seep out of him, as water from a cracked cup.

She bent low and gazed at his face. His mouth opened and he sighed very deeply.

"NO!" she cried out as she felt the last breath escape

his body. "I will not lose you, too."

His face was serene as the pain left him. Tara hugged him to her, sobbing fiercely, hoping by some miracle to infuse life into him. It was the hour before dawn and there was a pin-drop silence. Suddenly, she heard the clip-clop of hooves. A greenish light appeared at the mouth of the cave. Tara clutched Ananth tightly to her. As she stared at the mouth of the cave through tear-blurred eyes, she had a terrible premonition of what she was about to see. Lord Yama, the God of Death, stepped in. His enormous green body filled the cave and he carried a black mace slung over his shoulder.

"Let him go, Tara. Ananth is now mine."

"NO!" shrieked Tara. "He was fighting to save my life. You cannot take him. Bring him back to life."

"He is dead, Tara, and therefore mine. Give me his body and go your own way."

"NO! I am not leaving him."

Lord Yama got off the red bull and approached Tara.

"Stay away!" Tara yelled.

Lord Yama raised his hand, and Tara felt her strength drain away. Lord Yama gently lifted Ananth's body and walked to where the bull stood still, swishing its tail.

Tara hobbled after him and fell at his feet, begging and babbling.

"Please don't take him. This is the last person I have in the world. Please spare him. Someone, anyone, help me ..."

Lord Yama looked at her and the harsh lines on his face softened.

"Tara, death of a loved one is always hard to bear. There is nothing you or I can do. Be brave and get on with your life."

He got astride the bull and started to move away from her.

Tara jumped up. The story of Savitri and Satyaban flashed through her mind. She knew what she had to do. She followed the greenish glow and the sound of the bull's hooves out of the cave and down the steep mountainside.

Lord Yama heard her following and called out.

"Go back. You cannot follow us."

A cold wind froze the tears on her cheeks and numbed her hands and feet, but she kept walking.

"Go back, Tara. He is dead and you are not."

"If Savitri could follow her husband and get him back, then I can get my brother back," replied Tara. "I am *not* turning back. Do what you will."

"That was just a story, Tara, and stories do not come true. You are making me very angry."

With a roar, Lord Yama got off the bull and strode up to Tara. At each step he grew larger and looked more forbidding than ever with his green skin, his long hair, his stern expression, and his massive hands clenched into fists. He towered over Tara and brought his face inches away from hers and thundered,

"GO AWAY OR ELSE!"

Tara cowered before him. But she did not run away.

"Kill me and put me out of my misery," she yelled. "I do not want to live all alone. I have lost everyone I've loved. What is the point of my going on?"

She sank down on her knees, her body wracked with sobs. She heard Lord Yama walk away. The sound of the bull's hooves started up again. The chill in her heart overflowed and spread to the rest of her body.

Clop, clop, clop.

Silence.

Tara looked up, not daring to believe her ears. Lord Yama dismounted and came back to her. He knelt and stroked her hair.

"I can see that you are brave and loyal. Any other person would have run away, but you held your ground. You truly care about Ananth do you not?"

"He is my brother. I have already lost one. I'd rather die than lose another."

"I will give you a chance to win his life back. But it is going to be very tough. Are you prepared?"

"Yes," she said in a shaky voice. *What did he have in store for her?*

"There is a cave that leads deep down into the heart of the largest mountain in the Shivalik Hills: the Kailash Parbat. Your task is to bring back the Water of Life from a fountain in that cave. A few drops will restore Ananth to life. Tell me, Tara, will you do it?"

"Show me the way."

"The path to the fountain is guarded by many dark and evil things that have never seen the light of day. They will kill anyone who tries to get past them. There is no guarantee you will come back. I may then have to collect another body: yours!"

"I am ready, Lord Yama. I want to be with my brother, in life or in death."

"Such bravery in one so young! This deserves a fighting chance," he said, stroking his chin, speaking to himself. "I have met so many cowards and unscrupulous people lately that your loyalty and courage have touched my heart."

Tara stood still. Her heart was pounding so hard that the sound was deafeningly loud in her ears.

"Tara, listen to me carefully. I am going to give you some words of advice — three things that you must remember. You will have to decide how and when to use them. Remember them well, and perhaps they will save your life."

Tara nodded.

"The first is: People are not as they appear on the surface. Trust your heart, not your eyes."

Tara repeated it after him till she had memorized it.

"The second is: Sometimes the right way is the most difficult, while the wrong way, the most easy and tempting. Make your choice wisely."

Lord Yama looked at Tara as she repeated the sentence, her face screwed up in concentration.

"The third is: Help a person in need. You may end up

helping yourself.

"Do you remember everything?" he asked.

"Yes, Lord Yama, I do. Thank you for the chance to save my brother's life."

She walked toward the cave by his side as the sky in the distance started to lighten and the dawn chorus started. Lord Yama stopped and pointed to a deep, yawning hole in the mountainside.

"There's the entrance. Be careful. May the blessings of Lord Vishnu, the Preserver, be with you. Oh, and one more thing: you have twenty-four hours to return with the Water of Life. Even a minute after will be too late."

The Earth seemed to spin and a roaring filled Tara's ears. Twenty-four hours ... unnamed dangers ... three bits of advice and she all alone. She took a deep breath and the world slowed its spinning.

"May I say goodbye to Ananth?" she asked.

Lord Yama nodded and stepped aside.

Tara walked up to Ananth's body. In the soft light of dawn he looked so serene and peaceful. She leaned over and kissed his forehead.

"I'll return, Ananth, or I'll die trying. You gave your life to save me and now it's my turn. Sleep for a while, my brother. I *will* be back to wake you."

She turned back to the cave and started walking. Her body was icy cold. Panic had her heart in a firm grip.

"There is still time to say 'no,'" Lord Yama called out to her. "Once you step into the cave, there is no turning back. You will not be able to get out unless you have the Water of Life with you, or I come to collect your body."

Tara was unable to speak. She turned to look at Lord Yama one last time before she ran into the cave. The dark hole swallowed her up instantly, like black waters closing over the head of a drowning person.

CHAPTER 12
THE WATER OF LIFE

Tara's eyes adjusted to the gloom as she walked deeper and deeper into the cave, which slanted down at a steep angle. A smell of decay came off the slimy walls. The air was thick and seemed to have life of its own as it swirled around her. And then there was the deafening silence.

"I will save Ananth ... I will be successful ... I will save Ananth ...," she chanted to herself, not looking back at all. She knew she would run out if she glimpsed her freedom receding.

You can do this, you have to, she told herself. *This is your chance to save Ananth.* She remembered what her grandfather said to her often, especially at times when she was very scared:

"Tara, courage is not the absence, but the *mastery* of fear."

The fear was there — lots of it. Only the mastery was lacking!

As she talked to herself, the band that constricted her heart gradually loosened. She drew in a deep breath and felt calmer, panic retreating to a corner of her mind.

"SSSSSTTTTT," someone hissed in her ear. It echoed in the profound silence, and goose bumps rose on Tara's hands.

She stopped and reached out into the endless void. The inky blackness had sharpened her sense of hearing. Panic jumped back to centre stage. She thought her heart would explode.

"Who is there?"

All that came out of her throat was a strangled yelp. She tried again.

"Who is that? Show yourself!"

A faint outline began to form. Within minutes, an Apsara — a beautiful goddess — stood in front of her. She had luminous skin as if lit from within. Her shiny black hair fell to her shoulders. She wore a bright red saree, embroidered with sparkling golden threads and a bejewelled tiara. On her forehead, just where the arch of her eyebrows met, was a red dot outlined in gold that seemed to light up her serene face. Tara noticed that she had six hands instead of two, each holding a different item. One held a sceptre, one a golden pot, the third held a little mouse that sat patiently on her palm. Her fourth hand held a lamp and the fifth, a round, steel plate full of sweets. Her sixth hand was empty. A mesmerizing halo shimmered around her.

"Welcome, Tara. I have been waiting for you," she said

in a melodious voice.

"Do you know me?"

"I am a goddess. I know everybody and everything. You are here to get the Water of Life for Ananth."

"Yes."

"It is a long and tiring journey. Sit awhile and rest. I will give you food and water. Once you have regained your strength, you can go on."

Tara was entranced by the beauty and the soothing voice of the Apsara. She suddenly realized that it had been ages since she had eaten a decent meal. Her stomach growled as the goddess passed the plate of sweets in front of her nose and beckoned.

"Come with me, Tara, and I'll look after you."

Tara took a step forward, relieved that she would not have to go through this ordeal alone. She had panicked for nothing. Obviously, Lord Yama had not known about this friendly goddess. He had scared her for nothing with his grave expressions and his silly bits of advice. She almost laughed aloud with relief.

"Lead the way, Apsara. I am right behind you."

The Apsara turned and walked ahead, leading Tara deeper into the labyrinth of caves.

"Follow me."

At every step, the feeling that something was not right grew inside her like a large balloon. *I wish Ananth were here to guide me*, she thought. She was so undecided that her steps slowed.

"What is it, Tara? Surely you are not afraid of me? I am here to help you. You will perish without me," said the Apsara, her eyes flashing. "Come along now, it's not far. Don't delay or I am going to get angry."

The misgivings in Tara's heart blossomed. Lord Yama's words floated into her head, his voice gruff yet tinged with concern, "*People are not as they appear on the surface. Trust your heart, not your eyes.*" She had been so happy and relieved to have a companion on this dangerous quest — a goddess, no less. Yet her heart was very troubled.

Stop NOW, the voice inside her screamed. She continued walking, unsure of what to do.

Tara's eyes strayed to the little mouse clasped in the Apsara's hand. It sat there quietly, looking at her with an intense expression. She was surprised. She had never known a mouse to sit still. Suddenly, the mouse flopped over, exposing its belly. The sight made Tara shudder. It had no legs! The mouse could not run because it had *no legs*.

Who would do that to a small, defenceless creature? *A monster*, the little voice in her head said helpfully. And it added, in case she missed the point, she was following this "goddess" willingly. Who knows what fate would befall her if she, Tara, entered her home.

Her eyes darted left and right, trying to decide which way to run. The mouse seemed to understand her dilemma. It flicked its tail in the direction of a dark tunnel that was coming up on their right. Tara looked at the mouse in confusion. Its eyes seemed to bore into hers. It flicked its tail urgently, always pointing at her, at itself, and right, again and again and yet again. They were almost past the tunnel. Tara finally understood.

She grabbed the mouse from the Apsara's hand and dived into the tunnel the little creature had been frantically pointing to, then sprinted into the black void. Mud and slush underfoot made deep sucking sounds as she ran. She bounced off the walls and tripped over rocks as she hurtled blindly along the tunnel.

A shriek reverberated around her. The "goddess" had discovered that Tara was no longer following her. Tara heard thundering footsteps behind her. She turned back for a brief glimpse and her heart almost stopped beating. A massive monster pursued them. It was a pale yellow, as if suffering from a severe case of jaundice, with glowing, red eyes. Two white fangs stuck out from either side of the blood-red mouth. Its black, bushy hair flew back as it ran, resembling a nest of seething, writhing snakes. With a burst of energy, Tara sped up and ran for her life along the dark and endless tunnel.

"Turn right here," said the mouse in a strained voice, gasping for breath.

Tara realized that she had been squeezing the mouse so tightly she had almost suffocated it. She loosened her grip as she continued sprinting.

"Come here, Tara," said the monster. "I'll help you. Come here, my juicy little tidbit. I can almost taste your delicious flesh. Don't go."

Tara galloped faster.

"Left, right, left ... left, right," the mouse's voice came in staccato bursts.

Tara obeyed without thinking or seeing as her aching legs swerved left and right at top speed. Her breath came in ragged gasps and there was a painful stitch in her side. Her body was soaked and the acrid smell of her own sweat enveloped her. Her hands were starting to turn slippery, and she tightened her hold on her companion.

At long last, the monster's voice became fainter and then was altogether gone. Tara flopped down, panting heavily. Water from the damp floor seeped into her clothes and shoes, but she did not notice or care. She raised her hand and brought the mouse to eye level. His eyes glowed yellow so that she could see him faintly.

"Thank ... you," she gasped as she kissed its black button nose. "Who ... are ... you?"

"My name is Mushika."

Tara was shocked.

"But that is the name of ..."

"Yes," said the mouse. "I am Lord Ganesh's faithful servant. We meet again."

"Again? Have we met before?"

"You saved me from the cat not too long ago in the Ganesh temple in Morni. Do you not remember?"

"Yes. Now I do. But how did you get here?" asked Tara.

"Lord Ganesh was moved by your prayers and the hardships you have been through. He sent me here to wait for you. But that monster captured me and took away my legs using a powerful magic. You're the only one who can restore my legs, Tara. Lord Ganesh's power cannot penetrate this evil place. In return, I will guide you to the fountain."

"Thank you," said Tara, stroking the mouse. "Do you know how to get there?"

"Yes, but the way is extremely dangerous," said Mushika. "I'm not sure if you're strong enough to survive this."

"I have no choice. My brother's life is at stake. I cannot fail."

They sat for a few minutes in silence. Then Tara pushed herself up. Her legs shook and she almost fell over.

"Which way now?" asked Tara, gritting her teeth against the exhaustion that was spreading through her body.

"We have to go deep down to the heart of the Kailash Parbat. Be as quiet as possible. I'd rather not disturb any of the things that sleep here."

"What things?" asked Tara.

"The less you know, the better. Let's go," said Mushika.

Impenetrable blackness surrounded them and she was starting to feel its oppressive weight. Mushika's eyes glowed a deep yellow, casting a dim light in the thick gloom. The tunnel sloped downward. She took a deep breath, trying to shake off the feeling of claustrophobia in this close, dark place. They walked deeper and deeper and, with each step, Tara felt as if the entire weight of the mountain was pressing down on her.

Splash!

Tara had stepped into freezing water. Her foot was soaked all the way up to her ankle.

"OH!" She gasped and drew back her foot immediately. Mushika's eyes glowed brighter. Tara saw a large, black, underground lake stretched out in front of her. The water had an oily surface with barely a ripple on it.

"What should we do?" asked Tara, not liking the look of the water at all. Who knew how long this water had lain and what kind of dark, slimy creatures lurked in its turgid waters? She stood there chewing her lip, running a trembling hand through her hair.

"Surely there is another way to the other side," she said to Mushika, hope in her trembling voice.

Mushika shook his head.

"This is the only way. If we go any other way we may get lost, or encounter a danger far greater. We have to go on. Remember, time is running out. You have twenty-four hours to save Ananth. We do not have the luxury of a detour."

Tara closed her eyes as her imagination took over. What if there were water-snakes, or crocodiles with powerful jaws, or slimy monsters waiting to suck her down to the watery depths? What if the lake was endless and her strength gave way before she reached the other side? What if she drowned?

"Lord Ganesh, help me! I can't do this, I *can't*," she said as she sat down at the edge of the lake and sobbed.

"Don't cry, Tara. It's not that bad. Do you really want to try another way?" asked Mushika, moved by Tara's evident fear of the water.

She looked up hopefully. To their right, she could see a tunnel branching off upwards, toward light, toward air, toward freedom. She would go up and ask Lord Yama to spare Ananth's life. She would beg for his forgiveness at not having brought the water, but at least she would not be here, faced with the prospect of living out one of her worst nightmares. She looked back and forth between the black water and the path to freedom. The voice inside screamed *RUN*, but images of Ananth kept popping up in her head. Lord Yama's next piece of advice swam into her fatigued brain:

"*Sometimes the right way is the most difficult, while the wrong way the most easy and tempting. Make your choice wisely.*"

Tears slid down her cheek as the familiar downward-spiralling feeling of panic started, and she was powerless to stop it. She knew what she had to do. Time was running out; she had to go across the lake. Mushika snuggled up to her, squeaking encouragement. He, too, was worried, but trying not to show it. His little body shivered, and Tara could feel mini vibrations in her palm.

Tara saw a faint movement in the centre of that oily blackness and large ripples tiptoed lazily to shore. She stood up, shook her head, and straightened her shoulders.

"Lord Ganesh ... please look after us," she muttered, her heart thumping loudly in her ears.

She stepped into the water, which inched up her legs with icy fingers. It reached her ankles, then her knees. She forced herself to keep moving. She could already feel slimy things swirling around her, rubbing against her legs through the soaked cotton of her pyjamas. Every nerve was taut and frozen, but she forced herself to put one foot in front of the other, refusing to let panic take over. In she went, deeper and deeper, till the water was past her waist and creeping up to her neck and shoulders.

"Brave girl," squeaked Mushika, who was perched on Tara's shoulder. He was shivering so much in the icy air that rose from the surface of the lake that it seemed he might topple over. Finally, he decided to say no more. He dug his teeth into the collar of Tara's kurta and hung on. Mushika's eyes were like twin beams of faint light in that complete darkness. Tara's teeth were chattering as the intense cold seeped through her wet clothes and sucked out all the warmth from her body. Around her, the water swirled and churned. She heard splashes, gurgles, hisses. Something intertwined her legs and then slithered away. Bile rose in her mouth, but she clamped it shut and forced herself to keep going.

"Be ready to hop onto my head as soon as the water

reaches my shoulders," she told Mushika through clenched teeth.

Mushika squeaked.

The water reached Tara's shoulders and then it went no higher. Tara kept walking, expecting the ground to fall out from under her feet at any moment, but it never did. She had reached the deepest part of the lake and she realized she would not have to swim after all. She let out a deep, shaky breath. *Sometimes imagined horrors are so much scarier than the real thing*, she thought. She would have to remember this the next time.

The water was getting shallower. Without any warning, a huge, shapeless mass rose in front of her and a deep, dark smell of something malevolent took her breath away. In complete shock, she took a step backward, lost her balance and fell over. The murky, black water closed over her head. She blubbered in panic as she felt scaly things brush past her face and long, slimy creatures entwine themselves in her hair. The viscous water entered her mouth and nose, threatening to choke her. The foul taste made her gag. The world spun blackly. Ananth's body swam through her panicked mind and, with a Herculean effort, she stood up. She spit out the water, trying to control her heaving stomach.

Where was Mushika? He was no longer on her shoulder.

"Mushika!" she called out in a choked voice, fearful of losing her one companion and lifeline to sanity.

There was no answering squeak. And no light.

The darkness was so complete that she stood paralyzed for a moment, not knowing which direction to take. Suddenly, she was smothered in a wet, stinking blanket that was squeezing her so tightly she had difficulty breathing. She flailed her arms and legs, trying to get free. She tried to yell, but every time she opened her mouth she tasted rotten eggs and decayed fish. Tara decided to keep her mouth shut and concentrate on kicking free before she passed out completely.

It seemed useless. The blanket was getting snugger around her and the last of the air was disappearing. The blanket seemed heavier all of a sudden and Tara realized that it was slowly forcing her underwater. She sobbed as the water inched up her neck to her face, and she felt the last of the air vanish. She kicked with all her strength as her lungs cried out for air and panic surged through her body. Her foot connected with the blanket and then went through it — a hole. She dug her toe in and with all her strength pulled down. She heard a muffled ripping sound. She swam toward the rip, arms outstretched, black spots dancing in front of her eyes. She had a few seconds of consciousness left.

Swim ... swim through the tear, a voice told her, and she swam. Tara slipped easily through the tear and swam hard. Behind her, the shapeless mass thrashed wildly, searching for her. Tara surfaced and opened her mouth a moment too soon. The slimy water slid down her throat and, retching loudly, she vomited. Instantly, the shapeless mass drifted in her direction and she felt its edge curl around her foot. She stumbled away, hoping she was headed for shore.

The water level dropped at every step and she sobbed with relief. A long, scaly body wrapped itself around her foot, biting through the thin cotton. She kicked hard, and galloped out of the water.

Once on shore, Tara scrambled on all fours away from the water's edge and lay on the mud, panting. Then she remembered that Mushika was gone. A sob rose in her throat and her heart quailed at the thought of being lost in this darkness and finally going mad.

Sudden movements near her chest made her sit up with fear. Horrified, she tore at her kurta. She reached inside, grabbed the moving thing, and pulled it out.

"It's me, it's me," squeaked Mushika, shivering violently, coughing up water, and spraying Tara's wet face.

"I jumped down the neck of your kurta when you began to lose balance," he spluttered.

Tara took the little mouse in both hands and kissed its wet, furry head. Hot tears slid down her cheek.

"Thank Lord Ganesh you're still alive. I thought I had lost you."

"We have to move. That thing could come back," said Mushika.

Tara stood up as quickly as her numb body would allow her and hurried further away from the water. Dripping every step of the way, she walked down the tunnel leading away from the lake. The water splashed and thrashed behind her.

A gurgling erupted from the middle of the lake. Without a backward glance, Tara headed for the faint, red glow that emanated from the far end of tunnel. She squelched along it as fast as her cold and shaky legs would go. On her shoulder, Mushika squeaked encouragement, interspersed with sneezes.

"Good girl, Tara, aaaa-chhhoooo, keep going, don't stop now, aaaa-chhhoooo."

One of the sneezes was so violent that he toppled backward off her shoulder. Tara groped around on the floor till she found the sodden ball of fur. She picked him up tenderly.

"I think I'll keep you inside my pocket," she said. "It's wet, but at least I won't lose you."

Halfway down the tunnel they encountered a warm current of heat. Tara felt as if she was slowly sliding into a warm bath. Each step brought her closer to the warmth and she picked up speed as circulation returned to her frozen limbs. Steam was rising from her clothes. Mushika had stopped sneezing and she could hear a sigh of contentment as the warmth reached him, too. The heat increased as she got closer and so did the red glow that was starting to blind her.

From water into fire, thought Tara. The heat was intense now, and Tara was sweating profusely. Her clothes stuck to her skin. Perspiration beaded her brow and dripped into her eyes. She narrowed them to a slit against the glare.

At last, she reached the mouth of an enormous

underground cave. A huge pit of molten lava bubbled and hissed in front of her. It covered most of the floor of the cave leaving a narrow rim around the edge, leading to the far side.

"How are we going to cross this?" asked Tara aloud.

Despair and fear tinged her voice. The ledge was so narrow that one false step would cause her to plunge into that lava lake and be charred to a crisp in an instant. She sat listening to the angry spitting and crackling of the lava, tired beyond words. The scorching heat dried her tears before they reached her cheeks.

"This is just too much," she sobbed. "I'm so scared. How many more tests do I have to go through?" she called up at the black ceiling as if Lord Ganesh was sitting above her head, listening to her.

"Tara, what do you want most badly at the moment?" asked Mushika.

"To get out of here," she said.

"With or without the Water of Life?"

"Very funny, Mushika! Do you think I like wandering in the dark, playing with monsters and then running the risk of being cooked, for fun?" she snapped. "You know I am doing this for Ananth. He gave his life to save me and now I must save him."

"If you turned back, would you be able to forgive yourself?"

"No."

"Did you not survive the lake?"

Tara looked at Mushika's boot-button eyes and nodded.

"Even though you are very afraid, have faith in yourself. Focus on your goal and block out everything else that stands in the way. Especially panic, fear, and self-doubt. If your mind wants something badly enough, it will make your body do it. Remember that, Tara."

"What if I fall into the lava? What if I die?"

"Did you never play hopscotch or do tightrope-walking when you were a child?"

Tara gave a wry smile. "Lots of times, but I did not have a lake of molten lava under me."

"Okay, so focus on the path, ignore the lake, and keep your eye on the other side. You need the water. The only way to get there is around the lip of the cave. Let's go. Move, move, move!" commanded Mushika.

Before she could lose her nerve, Mushika had bullied Tara into stepping onto the narrow path. The lava bubbled and hissed mere inches away from her. Tara turned sideways so that her back was pressed against the wall and inched toward the far side, one agonizing step at a time. The lava gurgled and chortled as if mocking her feeble attempts at trying to avoid its hot embrace. Fierce heat scorched the soles of her feet. Sweat poured down her face and turned to steam so that she felt as if she would evaporate before she reached the other side.

"There you are, girl. Keep going," Mushika murmured in her ear.

She inched forward slowly. In the middle of the cave, Tara stopped. The lip had been so worn by the heat that it had crumbled, and there was a wide gap that she was going to have to step over. She stood there in utter defeat, fear and exhaustion making her teary. A cool breeze floated in from the tunnel beyond. A few short steps and she'd be out of this furnace. She closed her eyes and Suraj's image floated into her head. *You're brave Didi — you can do it*, he said. Ananth's face floated into her head. His silent form on Lord Yama's bull, waiting to be carried away to a place where he would sleep for an eternity ...

No! She was going to save him.

She clenched her fists, turned to face the gap, and stepped over the chasm. Then she inched sideways as fast as her shaky legs would allow her. Within a few moments, she had reached the far end of the cave, which branched off into another tunnel. She sank to the ground and crawled further into the tunnel, letting the cool air bathe her tortured skin.

Tara lay on the ground, breathing deeply. The relief of having crossed that hurdle was so great that for a moment her limbs seemed to have turned to jelly. She thanked every god she could think of.

"OOOF ... Get off, you're heavy," said a small, breathless voice.

Tara sat up immediately, realizing that she had been lying with her full weight on the little mouse.

"I'm so sorry, Mushika. We made it. WE MADE IT!"

Tara sprang up, clapping and dancing. She felt she could take on the world at this moment.

"I can see that," said the mouse sternly, recovering his breath and his humour. "It's not far to the fountain now. Let's not waste any more time and energy dancing. We have only two hours left."

Tara skipped down the dark tunnel, her heart light and joyous. A cool breeze caressed her face as she neared the end of the passage. A beautiful, silvery light shimmered in the distance and Tara was fascinated. On her shoulder, Mushika jiggled, and she could sense his impatience. As Tara neared the end of the tunnel, a sweet, soothing sound reached her ears. The silvery light brightened. Tara reached the cave and gasped in delight. Its high roof twinkled and sparkled and its walls shimmered. In the middle of the cave, a fountain of silvery water shot to the roof and cascaded as glistening stars to a pool at the base. Tara drank in the peace and beauty of the place greedily. The fragrance of roses perfumed the air, and acted like a balm on her tired body as she closed her eyes and took a deep breath. When she opened them again, everything had vanished. She stood in an empty cave surrounded by darkness.

"What is this, Mushika?" she called out in anguish and surprise. "Are we dreaming?"

"I don't know, Tara. I saw the fountain too, and now it's gone."

"There is more to this. I just know it," said Tara.

But this time there was just a flutter in her stomach and

168

not the numbing terror that she normally felt. Whatever came her way, she would face it. All of a sudden she felt a presence and turned around. A beautiful woman, clad in a white saree with intricate silver embroidery, stood there. She had light brown hair and fair skin.

"Who are you?" asked Tara.

"I am Maya, the guardian of the fountain. You are here for the Water of Life to save your brother, Ananth."

"Yes, but it was here a moment ago and now it's gone. Is this an illusion?"

"No, Tara," replied Maya. "The fountain exists and you saw a glimpse of it. But to see it again and get the water, you will have to pass my test."

"What do I have to do?" said Tara.

"Every person who makes it this far has to answer three riddles. If you can solve them, you can take the water. But if you fail, I will disappear and you will wander in these caves for an eternity."

Tara loved riddles, and this was a challenge that she *would* win. No goddess would be able to defeat her.

"I accept."

"What?" squeaked Mushika. "Are you mad? If you cannot answer all three, we are doomed."

"Are you ready?" asked Maya, arching one beautiful eyebrow.

"Yes," replied Tara.

"My first riddle is this:

A beautiful woman, stunning yet shy,
If she strikes you, you'll surely die.
No one knows how or why
Water can contain such fire."

Tara thought hard. Her mind ran through every possible riddle she had ever answered with Suraj and her mother. Something shimmered in her memory. A thunder cloud ... heavy rain, and ...

Mushika was squeaking in her ear "So ... do you know the answer or not?"

"I'm not sure."

"Not sure? *Not sure?* Tara, you'd better think hard. I want to see daylight again."

"So, Tara, do you know the answer?" asked Maya in a calm voice.

"Lightning," said Tara, clenching her fists.

"Correct."

Mushika heaved a sigh of relief and Tara relaxed.

"My next one is:

From dusk to dawn she stands and mourns.
Her hair is on fire, hot tears she weeps.
Grief melts her; all that's left is a heap."

Tara's mind was already whirring busily through the possibilities, while Mushika wriggled from her right shoulder to her left.

"So, Tara, can you answer this one?"

"Give me a few moments, Maya."

Tara was pacing, her stomach in a tight knot. This was a tough one. Her mother never made them this tough. Was she stupid to have taken the challenge? What if she couldn't answer? Not only would she be unable to save Ananth, but she would end up wandering around in this dark cave forever with no lamp or candle ...

"A candle, a candle!" she sang out.

"Correct!" said Maya, sounding a bit disappointed.

"Here is the last one, Tara. If you can answer this, the fountain will appear and the water is yours. Oh, and by the way, you have very little time left to get back to Ananth. No pressure," said Maya with a cold smile.

Tara kept her face expressionless, but her heart was hammering.

"Ask your last riddle."

"I see you and you see me,
Alike yet apart are we.
If another person should see,
I am he or she is me."

She waited in silence while Tara stared at her, stumped. She did not even know where to start. Her stomach contracted and her hands and feet were icy.

"Please, Maya. Could you repeat it one more time?" asked Tara in a quavering voice, hoping to buy some more time. Her head ached.

Maya repeated it again, a smile playing on her lips.

"Do you concede defeat?"

"NO WE DON'T!" squeaked Mushika. "Tara, let me help, let me help. Could it be bread? Elephant? Kettle? Monkey? Tree?" he started muttering.

"Quiet!" growled Tara. "I'm trying to think."

Her mind was a complete blank. *Think, think, think,* she told herself, *or you're stuck here forever.* She prayed to Lord Ganesh, clasped her hands together, and paced.

Maya was tapping her foot impatiently.

"Time is up!"

"Maya, please, just one more minute. I know the answer, I really do, I just can't remember it."

Maya relented, but an hourglass miraculously appeared in her hand and the sand started trickling through at a furious pace.

"One minute left, Tara. You'd better hurry up."

Tara was desperate. *Mother, where are you? If you had not disappeared, none of this would be happening.* But then her mother's words came back to her, a whisper in her ear. *"If you are ever sad, look into the mirror I gave you and you will find strength."*

Tara hastily pulled out the mirror pendant her mother had given her and glanced at the sand in the hourglass, hoping for a miracle. She gazed back at the mirror again and her eyes widened.

"Fifteen seconds left, Tara. I suggest you give up."

It was almost down to the last few grains and Mushika was swinging from her left earlobe in a panic.

"A MIRROR," she yelled as the last grain of sand fell.

Maya looked annoyed, but her anger soon passed and her face was calm again. All around them, the cave transformed. The silvery fountain reappeared. The water fell with a melodious, tinkling sound.

"Well done, Tara. You are the first person to have solved my riddles. But there is no time to waste. You have but a few minutes left. Ananth is waiting," said Maya.

From the folds of her saree she drew a glass bottle with a golden stopper.

"Take this bottle and fill it up. Give the first few drops to this brave little mouse here, and then give the rest to Ananth. He will be restored to life."

Tara took the proffered bottle. She ran to the fountain and held it out. Silver stars fell in and melted into clear water as the bottle filled up rapidly. Mushika sat on her shoulder, his eyes glinting with excitement. Tara lifted him from her shoulder and set him on the ground. Mushika opened his mouth eagerly and Tara poured in a few drops of the precious water. The moment the water slid down his throat, Mushika gave a violent shudder, flipped on his back, and lay still. Tara clapped her hand to her mouth in horror.

"Maya, what happened to Mushika? Is he dead? What did you make me give him? Is this the Water of Life or Death?"

She was babbling, but Mushika was so dear to her now

that she could not bear to be the one to have killed him.

"Patience, my child. Watch," said Maya.

Small pink stubs were poking out of Mushika's belly. As they watched, the legs elongated and little toes appeared. Within seconds, Mushika looked like a normal little mouse sleeping on his back. He opened his eyes and flipped over. Realization hit him instantly. He jumped, hopped, and ran around squeaking while Maya and Tara laughed at his antics.

"I must go. I want to see Ananth alive once again," said Tara.

She stooped to touch Maya's feet in a gesture of respect and profound gratitude.

"Bless you, my child; you are brave and intelligent," Maya told her. "I am very impressed with you. Take the tunnel from the far side of the cave — it will lead you straight to the entrance. And remember: do the right thing."

Tara, who was striding rapidly to the far end, heard the words and turned back, but Maya and the fountain had already vanished. What did she mean by that: "do the right thing"? And where had she heard this advice before? As Tara climbed the steep tunnel, she pondered the words. She was brought back to reality by a mouse who was determinedly practising mountain climbing on various parts of her anatomy.

"Stop that, you little idiot," she said as Mushika's feet dug into her neck, ears, and even her nose! "Enough already! You've gotten your legs back. They have to last you a lifetime, so don't wear them out already."

The air was starting to smell sweeter, bringing a promise of freedom and sunshine. Tara sprinted up in her eagerness to reach Ananth. Mushika held on for dear life.

"Slow down," he managed to squeak through clenched teeth.

"I can't! I want to reach Ananth before it's too late."

In the broadening daylight at the end of the tunnel Tara saw a bundle of rags. They seemed to be moving. She slowed down.

"What is that?" she whispered to Mushika.

"I don't know. Let's go closer, but be careful."

She strode up to the bundle, hoping against hope that this would not be another test. She clutched the bottle with the precious water to her chest. Drawing nearer, she saw that it was not a bundle of rags but a man writhing on the ground. A filthy, tattered kurta and pyjama covered his crumpled body. His long, dirty hair was matted and crawling with lice. His face was covered with grime, except where tears had streaked down his face, cutting a clear path through the filth. A small sound issued from his cracked, swollen lips. Tara knelt.

The man opened a puffed eye, caked with white mucous, and muttered, "Water ..."

Tara leaned closer. He looked ill and stank strongly of urine. Tara tried not to wrinkle her nose in disgust.

"Baba, I have something that I must do. I'll be back very soon with water and help."

"NO!" he croaked. "Help ... now. What's ... in ... your hand?"

A solitary ray of sunshine had found its way into the tunnel. It lit up the bottle of water clenched in Tara's hand. The beggar had forced open both eyes and was now looking at the bottle as his pleading continued.

"Water ... I don't ... want ... to die."

Tara looked at him in dismay.

"Not this water, Baba. This is for my brother, Ananth, who is lying dead in the clutches of Lord Yama. This water will bring him back to life."

"Water ... *please*."

His voice trailed into an exhausted croak. His eyes closed and he lay still.

"What should I do, Mushika? I can't go back in to get more water. Baba will die if I leave him. If I give it to him, I have lost Ananth forever. What should I do?" She chewed her lower lip ferociously.

Lord Yama's words came back to her: "*Help a person in need. You may end up helping yourself.*"

"Do the right thing, Tara." Mushika's words made her look up: he'd said exactly what Maya and Lord Yama had said to her earlier. She looked at the sick man. She looked back at the tunnel and all the horrors she had experienced in there. Could she turn away from a living person to bring someone back from the dead? If this was right, why did it take so much effort? What about Ananth? After all this, was she to lose him forever?

The old man raised a trembling hand to her in mute appeal. She saw the wrinkles, the thick, blue veins that criss-crossed under his pale skin. The hand fell back and he was still. Tara made her decision. She uncorked the bottle and raised the old man's head into her lap.

"Open your mouth, Baba. Here is the water."

She tilted his head back and poured the water down his throat. As the water slid out in a silvery stream, it seemed like all the happiness was draining out of her body. She stood up in a daze of pain. Ananth's dead body swam into her mind's eye and her eyes filled with tears, blurring her sight. *Ananth, I am so sorry I could not save you. I had to save Ba—*

"Tara," said a familiar voice.

Her eyes snapped open. Ananth stood in front of her, grinning from ear to ear. He rushed to her and gave her a hug. She stood there, sobbing. Mushika sat on her shoulder and wept, too.

"That old man was you?" she said.

Ananth nodded.

Lord Yama appeared at the mouth of the cave and beckoned to both of them.

"I am so proud of you, Tara. You remembered all my instructions and followed them. Your heart is as pure as you are brave. This was the last test to see if you would let someone die for the selfish purpose of bringing your brother back to life. You are true to your name: 'Tara,' which means 'star.' You are a guiding light to all who know

177

you. If you ever need my help, blow into this shell and I will be there," he said, handing her a pearly white conch shell with a pale pink edge.

"And there are your things," he said, pointing to their bundles at the mouth of the cave.

Tara folded her hands and bowed her head. She took the shell from him and tucked it into her pocket. Lord Yama mounted his bull, clip-clopped off into the trees, and vanished.

Laughing and crying at the same time, Tara clasped Ananth's hand, not daring to believe she had survived the journey and brought her brother back to life. Hope and confidence surged through her body and she felt happier than she had in a long, long time.

"Tara, you did it, *all alone*. I am impressed. It feels so good to be alive again."

"I did have some help. This is Mushika."

She held out her right hand where Mushika sat, nose woffling, bright, black eyes glinting. Ananth stroked his head.

"So, this is your little guide. Thank you, Mushika! Tara, you have given me a new life and it is pledged to you till we can find your mother and grandfather."

Tara's heart was bursting with joy as they walked away from the cave. She had fought against a situation that most people would have considered hopeless and *won*. She had brought Ananth back from the dead. She felt up to any challenge now. And she had gained a new friend, who now lay fast asleep in the inner pocket of her kurta.

"Zarku will not take long to find out that we are still alive. The attack on us will be swift and soon," said Ananth in a serious voice. "Let's get to that temple, Tara. Our lives, and the lives of all the villagers, will depend on how quickly we can find Prabala and bring him back to Morni."

Tara quickly located the twin peaks in the Shivaliks, between which the temple lay, and headed for them. It was late afternoon and the sun was already losing heat. Black clouds sailed past its face, heralding a stormy night ahead.

"Let's find a safe place for the night and we can decide what to do tomorrow," said Tara. "I am so tired I could sleep right here," she continued with a loud yawn.

They walked in silence, keeping a lookout for shelter. Mushika had woken up and was perched on Tara's shoulder, scanning the path along with her. He squeaked and his long tail whipped up and pointed. The path they walked on hugged the mountain on the right. The road fell away to a steep valley on the left. Far below in the waning daylight they could see many people clumsily climbing the slopes. There was no mistaking their greenish hue and dark hair.

"Vetalas. They're searching for us," said Ananth.

CHAPTER 13
PARVATI

Mushika's sharp eyes spotted a crevice in the mountain as they walked past.

"There," he squeaked in excitement.

Ananth and Tara stopped to examine the narrow fissure in the rock. It seemed big enough for both of them to squeeze through. But would there be any place to sit and rest?

"Let me take a look," said Ananth.

He squeezed inside. Tara stood outside, rubbing her arms to keep warm. Her eyes focused on the valley below. It was impossible to see anything in the gloom. She looked up. Stars adorned the night sky as if someone had carelessly scattered diamonds on a black carpet.

"Well, what do you see?" asked Tara, after a few moments.

"It's very narrow, but deep," called out Ananth. His voice sounded hollow and muffled.

"Hurry up. I'm freezing," said Tara.

There was no reply from Ananth. Suddenly, a green hand shot out from the crevice and grabbed her wrist. Tara shrieked in panic and, snatching her hand away, sprinted up the path. Laughter reached her and she stopped. She whirled back in anger as she recognized the voice.

"You, you ... stupid idiot," spluttered Tara, stomping back to him.

"I'm sorry," Ananth said as he squeezed out of the crevice covered with green moss. "I couldn't resist."

The dangerous gleam in Tara's eyes stopped any further joking.

"This crevice is quite deep, and at the very back is a small cave," continued Ananth. "If we collect firewood, we could light a small fire."

"That's a stupid idea," said Tara in a cold voice. "The smoke will give us away. I have a couple of blankets. We can use those."

"I'm sorry, Tara. I didn't mean to scare you. Can't I even tease my sister?"

Tara looked at his mischievous eyes glinting in the moonlight. She was suddenly reminded of Suraj.

"All right, but don't do it again."

They both squeezed into the crevice with the bundles. Mushika zipped through their legs and was in before them. The cave at the back was small but cosy. They unpacked the blankets and huddled close to wait out the night.

A blood-curdling howl sounded in the distance and

Tara clasped Ananth's hand tightly. The minutes limped past and it seemed that the night would be endless. There was nothing to see or do in the complete darkness. The only sound was the occasional rumbling of empty stomachs. Mushika pattered over her shoulders and snuggled against her cheek.

"It's too silent," said Ananth after a long while had passed. "Should I go take a peek?"

"No! You stay right here," hissed Tara.

"Let me," said Mushika. "No one will see me."

"Go, but be careful," said Tara.

Mushika ran out of the cave silently. Time crawled wearily by and Tara was starting to get really anxious when Mushika did not return.

"Why is he taking so long?"

"Be patient, Tara, he's just a small mouse. The distance you can cover in a step, he probably needs fifty. He'll be back," said Ananth, patting her arm.

No sooner were the words out of his mouth when Mushika shot into the cave, panting hard. He dived straight into Tara's lap and sat there quaking.

"They're he-here," he stammered.

"Who?" whispered Tara and Ananth in unison, though they both knew the answer.

"The Vetalas! There are so many of them. They're marching up the hillside, checking every bush and tree and rock. There is a tall, bald man in black who is leading them. He's been yelling at them to find and kill you both."

183

Mushika jumped straight into the inner pocket of Tara's kurta. His terror touched her heart. Tara wished she too could nestle up in someone's arms: her mother's.

The sound of an advancing army reached their ears — closer and closer they marched. Tara flattened herself at the back of the cave, the thump of her own heartbeat deafeningly loud in her ears.

"Find them and kill them TONIGHT," said a harsh voice, vibrating with suppressed anger.

Zarku's voice. They were doomed.

"Oh Mother, where are you? Please, help us," Tara prayed aloud.

"I am here, my child," said a soft voice from behind her. "Did you think I'd abandon you in your hour of need?" Tara peered into the inky depths of the black cave in shock. She heard a slithering sound.

"Mother? Is that really you?" she asked, not daring to believe her ears. "Where are you?"

Ananth groped for the matches in the bundle and drew out the box. He lit one and held it up.

"Here," said the voice, and into the dim light slithered a black cobra. The markings on its hood and shiny scales glistened in the match light.

Tara instinctively drew back. She hated snakes, and cobras most of all.

"It's me, Tara. Don't be afraid," said the cobra, spreading its fan, tasting the air.

Tara stopped and gazed at the snake in amazement.

This was the same snake she had seen days ago in their hut in Morni. This snake had kissed Suraj and herself that night.

"Mother, it was you all along. You were close to us and watching over us. You didn't abandon us after all."

"Yes, my darling child. But there is no time to talk right now. Your lives are in great danger. Zarku will kill you if he finds you. We have to run."

Tara scrambled to her feet, ready to bolt out of the cave.

"Not that way, Tara. Zarku is already at the entrance."

"Then how ...?" asked Tara, looking from Ananth to the cobra in confusion.

"You have to trust me, both of you. I'm going to bite you to transform you into snakes so we can slip away unseen."

Tara crawled forward, but Ananth stopped her.

"How do we know this is not a trick of Zarku's to flush us out?"

Tara hesitated. She hadn't thought of that.

"Trust me, Tara. It is *I*, your mother. In a few moments it will be too late. You have left so many footprints at the entrance of the cave that Zarku will have no difficulty finding you."

"Mother, what did you give me the night you disappeared?" asked Tara in a breathless voice.

"The triangular mirror on a golden chain, and I told you to keep it with you, always."

"It is Mother," wept Tara in relief. "No one else could have known that."

She crawled forward and stretched her face toward the black cobra, her eyes squished shut. She felt a pinprick on her throat and gasped. The next instant, a fiery sensation traced a searing path through her veins. She felt her body twisting and shrinking upon itself. She looked down and saw that she had turned into a smaller replica of her mother. Tara raised her hood and looked around. Her eyesight was crisp and clear. Next to her she saw a slightly larger cobra: Ananth.

"Quick, follow me and be absolutely quiet," said Parvati. "Mushika, come with us."

She glided out of the crevice but instead of crawling out onto the path, she went up the wall, which was overgrown with vines, and onto the branch of a sal tree. Tara and Ananth followed her into the safety of the leaves. Mushika scampered up behind them, sure-footed and confident. From their perch, they watched silently.

Zarku stood at the entrance, pointing to the footsteps. The rest of the Vetalas stood around him, holding aloft burning torches.

"Both of them are in there. SEIZE THEM NOW," roared Zarku, his third eye spitting yellow sparks. Two of the thinnest Vetalas came forward and squeezed through the crevice while the others surrounded the entrance.

Tara moved closer to her mother. Needing her touch, she intertwined the tip of her tail with her mother's tail.

Their sleek black bodies blended in with the foliage, making them invisible.

"Hurry up, you morons. What is taking so long?" yelled Zarku. "Drag them out here so that I can have the pleasure of burning them to ashes."

Within minutes, the Vetalas reappeared. Heads bowed, they inched toward Zarku, trembling from head to foot. One of them pointed into the cave and grunted, shaking his head.

"NO NO *NOOOOOOO*," yelled Zarku. "They have escaped yet again, and you imbeciles have let it happen. You will be severely punished," he said, his voice dropping to a whisper.

Both Vetalas threw themselves onto Zarku's feet, mewling for mercy. Zarku looked down at them. His face was expressionless but his black eyes were twin whirlpools of rage.

His third eye, spitting red sparks, opened fully. The beam expanded to bathe the Vetalas cowering at his feet. The men on the ground shrieked in pain and terror. The rest of the army stood back in mute horror. The beam intensified. The skin of the two Vetalas started to blister and the smell of burnt flesh filled the air. Their hair caught fire and their eyeballs melted and dripped down their faces in rivulets of black. Tara closed her eyes and tried to drown out the agonized howling. Within seconds, the men were reduced to a pile of grey ash. Zarku jumped into the pile with both feet and did a manic dance, scattering the ashes in all directions as he giggled. Then, he stopped.

"As for the rest of you," he said, addressing the survivors, "go find the children and bring them to me, dead or alive, or else ..."

He swivelled on his heel and walked away.

There was a long silence. Tara wept and gazed at the Vetalas, who stood staring at the scattered ashes in shock.

"Come on, we have a long way to go," whispered Parvati.

"Are we going to the Devi Temple, Mother?

"No, Tara, we're going to a cave at the top of this mountain. It's closer and safer."

She slithered higher up the tree. Tara followed her gracefully, revelling in the fluid movement without fear of being discovered. Ananth followed her. They made their way up to the summit of the mountain, racing from tree to tree. Mushika kept pace with them.

After what seemed like hours, Tara was absolutely exhausted. "How much further, Mother? I am so tired. Can't we rest?"

"Just a little further, Tara! Don't you want to see Suraj?"

"Suraj? Is he alive?" Her heart swelled with joy. "But when he disappeared ... I thought that wild animals had ... how?"

"Wait and see."

Energy coursed through Tara's supple frame.

"I have so much to ask you, Mother."

"I have much to tell you, Tara."

Ananth was silent.

"I have a surprise for you, too, Ananth," said Parvati.

"I've lost both my parents. No surprise could bring me joy," he replied in a flat voice.

"We'll see about that," said Parvati.

Dawn was breaking as all four of them reached the cave. A large banyan tree stood outside it. Parvati slid down a swaying root and vanished into the depths of the cave, followed closely by Mushika. Tara waited for Ananth to catch up. He was very slow.

"What's the matter, Ananth? Something is wrong, and you had better tell me what it is or we are not going any further."

"I miss my mother," he said in a choked voice. "Seeing your mother reminded me of mine."

Tara slithered up to him and looked him in the eye.

"I will share my mother with you. I am sure she would be happy to accept you as her child. Suraj and I would love to have an elder brother."

"It will not be the same," he said in a gruff voice. Nevertheless, he sounded happier.

"Now, let's go in. I am dying to see Suraj. You'll love him, but he can be quite silly ..."

Babbling on and on, Tara led the way and they slid into the cave just as the sun peeped over the horizon. Parvati was nowhere to be seen. In the gloom, Tara saw a man coming toward her, but she could not see his face. He was too big to be Suraj. She stopped. As he came nearer she noticed the stick in his hand. A trap! This man was coming to kill them!

"RUN!" she screamed as she whirled round.

Ananth was right behind her and, in their haste, their bodies tangled together and they writhed on the floor helplessly, unable to escape. The man came toward them rapidly. His stick swished through the air. She flinched and waited for the blow to land on her head, certain that death would be instantaneous.

CHAPTER 14
MAGIC IN THE MOUNTAINS

Tara felt a light tap on her head. She raised her hand to her head and felt hair — she had changed back into her human form. She looked at Ananth, who lay sprawled on the floor next to her. As her eyes adjusted to the gloom, she recognized the face staring down at them. Her grandfather, Prabala, stood there, tears streaming down his face, his arms outstretched.

"Come here, Tara."

He gathered her close in a warm embrace.

"I have missed you so much, my child. You have been through a lot these past few days. Yes," he said, sensing her astonishment. "I know everything."

Tara hugged him back with equal intensity. Ananth stood close by without saying a word.

"Ananth, come here. You have been extremely brave and a great help to Tara." Prabala drew Ananth into his embrace. Tara was feeling safe for the first time in ages and was reluctant to let go.

"Where is Mother, Dada?" she asked Prabala, addressing her grandfather respectfully.

"She is preparing a meal for all of us."

Prabala uttered a few words. A huge stone rolled itself in front of the cave, sealing the entrance. Then he put an arm around Tara and Ananth and led them to the back of the cave, where a welcoming fire crackled. Tara gasped and Ananth's mouth fell open in surprise. There sat his mother, Gayatri, with another woman and a little boy.

"Mother!" he yelled, running forward and embracing her.

Tara saw Suraj that same instant and he catapulted himself into her arms. She covered him with kisses.

"My baby brother! You're alive, you're safe!"

"Who are you calling a baby?" he demanded, yet he snuggled deep into her arms.

Everyone cried and spoke at the same time. Prabala raised his hand and said, "One at a time, please."

"Suraj, what happened to you? How did you get here?" asked Tara. She closed her eyes, the memory of his disappearance still very painful, even though she could see Suraj was alive and well.

"A lot happened, Didi. But it is a long story."

"Children," boomed Prabala, "let's eat and then we'll talk. I know both of you have a lot of questions," he said, looking at Tara and Ananth.

Amid laughter and tears, everyone sat down to a delicious meal. Tara had forgotten what a hot meal tasted like. Parvati and Gayatri had prepared a feast that belied the ascetic setting of the cave. There was succulent wild fowl simmered in a spicy butter gravy, roast hare with tandoori masala, hot rice flavoured with cumin seeds, and yellow dal with ghee.

The aromas wafted around them, making everyone's mouth water. Before she started eating, Tara put a bit of everything on a leaf and offered it to Mushika, who sat patiently behind her, emitting tiny squeaks now and then. For a while, there was complete silence as everyone piled their banana leaves high with the dal, rice, wild fowl, and hare. Ananth, Tara, and Suraj slurped and burped their way through the meal, sighing deeply from time to time. At last, everyone finished eating and Parvati cleared away the banana leaves and brought out some paan, which she distributed to the elders; the children had sweet rice pudding. Tara was feeling full and drowsy, but questions were whizzing around in her mind. Ananth's mother made them all a hot cup of tea and they sat round a cosy fire to catch up on all the news.

"Where have you been all this while, Mother?" asked Tara.

Parvati's eyes became misty, and, clearing her throat, she began.

"After the villagers decided that I was a witch and I was to be stoned to death, I knew I had to escape. Father and I both decided to go away for a while. I knew that we would be needed by Morni later, much later, and we had to stay alive to save the villagers from the clutches of Zarku."

"You saw this happening, didn't you?" said Tara.

Parvati nodded.

"But why did you not tell us?" snapped Tara, her eyes flashing, her voice strident. "Why did you let us think you had disappeared forever or worse, died? That was a very cruel thing you did to us, Mother."

"How could I do otherwise, my child?" said Parvati, stroking Tara's hair. "No one could know. If you had known, Zarku or Kali would have tortured you till they made you tell the truth. But I was always watching over you. Always! On Diwali night, I could not restrain myself and I came out of hiding and kissed both of you. Do you remember?"

"Mother was that snake," said Suraj, unable to keep quiet.

Tara remembered it vividly. She had already recognized her mother when she'd come to rescue them from Zarku. This is why they had survived — why Bela had licked her cheek; she had known it was Parvati watching over them.

"Father turned me into a snake so I could see both of you," continued Parvati. "I missed you so much. I was able to inject some of my powers into you so that you would know when you were in danger. You'd see an image that would warn you. Do you remember?"

Tara nodded as many things started to make sense.

"When the two of you escaped into the jungle, I followed you, keeping a safe distance."

"The black cobra that saved Suraj from the python — that was you," breathed Tara in awe. "You saved Suraj's life."

"Yes."

"Oh Mother, how could I *ever* have doubted you?"

She hugged her mother, breathing in the smell of her and feeling calm and safe in her arms.

"But then Suraj fell ill after we got caught in that rain shower," said Tara, sitting up again as the thought occurred to her.

"Yes, I know. I saw you struggle to keep him alive. But he was getting worse. He needed more advanced medicine than you knew how to make. That is when your grandfather and I decided to take him with us and nurse him to health."

"And you left me all alone. How could you do that? Don't you love me as much as Suraj?" asked Tara, her face blotched with colour at the memory of the pain and despair she had felt when she thought Suraj had died.

"Hush, child," said Prabala. "Don't speak to your mother that way. There was a reason."

Parvati looked anguished and very hurt at Tara's outburst. Tears leaked out of her eyes and she wiped them away with the edge of her blue and gold saree.

"What reason could there possibly be?" yelled Tara.

She stood up and stamped her foot on the ground, raising a puff of dust.

"Do you know the pain I went through, thinking that I had lost my mother and then my brother? Do you know how much I blamed myself for having failed him? I'm furious with all of you for doing this, and *you* most of all, Mother."

A sob escaped Parvati. Tara whirled on her heel and was about to stomp away when Prabala spoke up.

"Tara, I am going to tell you a story and then you decide whether your mother and I did the right thing. Please sit down and listen to me."

Tara turned and stood with her hands folded over her chest, glowering at them.

"There was once a little boy who saw a butterfly emerging from its cocoon. The hole in the cocoon was extremely small and the butterfly struggled for hours to get out. It seemed to be making no progress at all. After some time it stopped to rest. The little boy felt extremely sorry for it and, taking a sharp knife, he slit open the cocoon. The butterfly emerged easily, but its wings and body were tiny and shrivelled. The boy had crippled the butterfly for life by helping it out of the cocoon. It was never able to fly. The struggle was Lord Brahma's design to strengthen the butterfly's wings so that when it finally got out of the cocoon using its own strength, it would be ready to take flight."

Tara was enthralled by the story, but she maintained

her sulky expression.

"What has that got to do with me?" she asked.

"My child," said Parvati in husky voice, "this was our way of making you strong; of allowing you the opportunity to strengthen your spirit. It was very, very difficult, but I had to do it, for your sake."

"You used to be such a coward when you knew that you always had someone to look after you and who you could rely on," said Prabala. "Could you have braved the dangers in the cave to bring Ananth back to life, before your mother disappeared? Just look at yourself now and tell me if the last few days have not made you stronger than ever before."

It seemed as if someone had lifted the huge rock that was crushing her heart. This was all part of their plan. They knew she would meet Ananth and that the hardships she'd endure before reaching them would strengthen her. No one could have helped her become the person she was today. If they had rescued her along with Suraj, she would again have come to rely on her mother and grandfather for help. She gazed at all the faces around the fire and was warmed by the pride she saw there.

She walked back to Parvati and sat down beside her, head bowed.

"I am very sorry, Mother. I understand now. Your actions forced me to look inward rather than outward for strength. Will you forgive me?"

Parvati kissed the top of Tara's head.

Ananth spoke up.

"Mother, how did you get here? The last I saw of you ...," he fell silent and clutched her hand tightly.

"Prabala, disguised as a tiger, saved me from those merciless villagers who were going to burn me on my husband's funeral pyre," said Gayatri in a choked voice. "I wanted to live — for you, my son. I am so sorry for the pain and anguish you have been through. Thanks to Tara you have returned to me. We are both very lucky."

Tara now understood what had really happened. She was glad she had spared Ananth the pain of believing his mother had been eaten by a tiger.

Parvati continued.

"We brought Suraj back and nursed him back to health, but all of us kept a watch on you, waiting for the time when you would have the strength to face the biggest ordeal yet."

Tara turned pale as she gazed at Prabala.

"Yes, Tara, you know what I mean," said Prabala. "We have to rid Morni of Zarku and Kali. We have to free all those poor souls that make up his army of Vetalas. But it's not going to be easy. They are both very evil and will put up a good fight. Kali had Zarku hypnotize your father. This is why he never said a word, even though she ill-treated both of you."

"And tried to kill us," said Suraj with a grimace.

Parvati looked very grave. "It is due to the mercy of Lord Ganesh that both my children escaped death time and time again."

"You are a good woman, Parvati," said Prabala. "Your good deeds and all the kindness you have shown to the villagers were rewarded and that is why your children escaped death."

Tara nodded. "Lord Ganesh sent Mushika to help me."

Mushika, who was still nibbling rice from a small portion of the banana leaf, looked up and said, "Now that you are safe, it is time I went back to my master."

Tara kissed his nose and stroked his back gently. He flicked his tail in farewell and disappeared.

"How do we kill Zarku?" asked Ananth. "The people of our village have seen the wrath of his third eye," he said, shuddering.

"I have seen it, too," said Tara, looking extremely fearful. "That ray from his eye turns people to ash, but not before it scorches their flesh and burns them alive. He enjoys watching them die a horribly painful death. The louder they scream, the more he giggles!"

"Father, we must do something to save the villagers," said Parvati.

"I'd like to show all of you something special," said Prabala.

Instantly, everyone was quiet, staring at him.

Prabala held out his palm. On it lay a gnarled, brown seed through which was strung a black, cotton thread. Prabala gazed at it reverently.

"What is that seed, Dada?" asked Tara.

"My reward for years of penance and devotion to the gods Brahma, Vishnu, and Shiva — the holy Trinity."

"You didn't do a very good job, did you Dada?" said Suraj with a wry expression, "if all they gave you was a dry seed."

Prabala threw back his head and roared with laughter. Suraj joined in without knowing why.

"This is no ordinary seed, children," he said, looking around. "It is the rudraksha; a gift from the gods. When I tie it on my arm, it infuses me with strength, wisdom, and courage. And most of all, immunity against evil influences."

There was silence.

"This little seed can do all that?" asked Ananth.

"Yes," said Prabala. "But it must be tied to my right arm at all times. Without it, my powers are weak."

"So then, let me tie it on your arm, Dada, and let's go back to Morni right away," said Tara, jumping up.

"Patience, my child," said Prabala. "We must wait for Soma, the Moon God, to appear. He will be at full strength tonight. We will say a prayer in his honour. At night, the Moon God reigns the sky, and if we have his blessing, we can conquer anything and anyone. Get some sleep today, because tonight is our final test."

CHAPTER 15
SOMA

Tara woke a few hours later to the fragrance of tea, freshly cooked chappatis, and rice kheer. For a moment, she thought she was back in Morni. As she came fully awake, she realized she was safe with her mother and grandfather in a cave in the heart of the Shivalik Hills. Her beloved brothers Suraj and Ananth were close by. She lay there smiling to herself in the darkness, watching the flames. Content, she stretched like a cat and yawned. The very next minute, all the breath was knocked out of her.

"OOOOF," she gasped as a large, heavy object landed squarely on her stomach.

"Suraj! Get off me," yelled Tara, pushing her brother off.

He clung to her like a leech, making weird faces. They punched each other in a mock battle. As Tara rolled on the floor, the mirror she wore fell out. It sparkled orange with the reflection of the flames.

"Good girl, you still have it with you," said Parvati, stooping to look at the exquisite, triangular mirror.

"It was your last gift to me before you disappeared," said Tara, sitting up. "Do you remember what you said when you gave it to me?"

"Wear it always and look into it whenever you need strength," said Parvati.

"I have looked at it often these last few days," said Tara.

"Tara, there is more to the necklace than just pretty stones. Do you want to hear it?" asked Parvati, stroking the stones lovingly with her thumb.

Tara nodded. Parvati sat down next to Tara with her feet folded gracefully to one side.

"The three sides of the mirror represent the highest of the Hindu God Trinity: Brahma, Vishnu, and Shiva. Together they represent the heaven, the earth, and the underworld."

Tara was entranced once again by the beauty of the necklace. Suraj and Ananth had also gathered round and were listening intently to Parvati's explanation.

"Now, see these stones? The round red stones represent the sun — Suraj — and the blue, star-shaped stones represent ..."

"The stars ... me," piped in Tara with a smile on her face.

"Yes, you, my beloved Tara. This necklace is a representation of my most precious belongings in this world: the two of you, my star and my sun," said Parvati. "This necklace was blessed by Lord Ganesh during a sacred prayer ceremony conducted by your grandfather so that no matter what, both of you would always be protected. Now you see why I left it with you?"

"Attention," called out Prabala, who had come up to them. "We have a lot to do before we go back to Morni."

There was immediate silence.

"We will go to Morni tonight," he said, the wrinkles on his forehead more pronounced than ever.

"Zarku intends to make his final and most deadly move tonight. I can feel it. Tonight, he plans to put all of Morni under his spell. I will not let it happen. MORNI IS MINE!"

Tara stared at her grandfather in amazement. She had never heard him speak like this before. He almost sounded like ... and she stopped. *Zarku*, the voice inside her completed. She ignored it.

"First of all, let us pray to the gods for their help and their blessings," said Prabala.

Parvati had put together prayer offerings in a copper plate: milk, fruits, and flowers. Prabala took the plate from her and they all trooped to the cave entrance. Prabala uttered a few words and the stone in front of the cave rolled away, letting in the cold and crisp night air. They followed Prabala to the clearing outside. He raised the plate to the sky and murmured a prayer under his breath.

Everyone was silent behind him, heads bowed and hands

folded in prayer. Prabala took some holy water from a small copper cup and sprinkled it in the air. Soma, the Moon God, emerged from the dark horizon in full splendour. He beamed at the group in front of him. Prabala supplicated himself in front of Soma and the others followed suit. Soma glowed brighter, accepting their prayers, and bathed them in a crystal clear light. The next moment, everything went black, though there was not a single cloud in the sky. It seemed as if some powerful force had extinguished the moon.

"What happened?" asked Tara. "Is Soma angry with us? Did we do something to annoy him, Dada?"

"No, Tara," answered Prabala. "Soma is showing us what he can do. He will give us light when we need it and darkness when we don't."

A single beam of moonlight shot out of the darkness and touched Prabala's forehead. He bowed to Soma once again.

"Let's go," he said, rising. They all filed back into the cave.

"Parvati, can you see what is happening in Morni? Something is very wrong," said Prabala as he paced the length of the cave.

"No, Father. Every time I try to picture the village, there is a grey fog that seems to shroud it."

"Zarku has indeed become very strong. He has been capturing the souls of all the villagers he's hypnotized. I am sure that he has made Kubera, the Lord of the Underworld, very happy. They have been feeding each other with power," said Prabala, wringing his hands.

"Don't worry, Father. I am sure you will be more than a match for him. You are the best healer ever. And you have the blessings of the gods," she said.

She smiled at him, confidence radiating from her beautiful face. Prabala smiled back.

"What about Lord Yama?" asked Tara. "Isn't he going to be angry that he has been cheated out of the souls of the dead?" she asked Prabala.

"I am sure he must be very angry. But Kubera is very happy with Zarku at the moment. Zarku is feeding him with live souls, making him extremely powerful. Lord Yama can only claim the dead. This makes him less useful to Kubera right now."

Prabala continued his pacing, muttering under his breath while everyone prepared for their journey into Morni.

• • •

Tara stole out of the cave unseen. She emerged into the cold night. Bright stars twinkled overhead and the moon shone from a corner of the sky. She slipped the conch shell out of her pocket and put it to her mouth. The cold shell against her warm lips made her shiver. She took a deep breath and blew hard. The sound of a hundred waves crashing onto the shore ensued from it, startling her. She looked around to see if anyone had heard it. She expected Ananth to come racing out. No one came. *Maybe Lord Yama and I are the only ones who can hear it*, she thought.

She blew into the shell again. This time a silvery tinkle floated out. It was beautiful and soothing. Still, no one heard it and there was no sign of Lord Yama.

She blew into it a third time and the sound of a hundred galloping horses erupted from the conch. She almost dropped the shell in surprise. The night seemed undisturbed.

Tara stood alone at the edge of the clearing. Was this a joke Lord Yama had played on her? There was no sign of him. Her eyes searched the dense foliage for signs of life. Nothing stirred. Her shoulders sagged and she headed back to the cave.

Clip-clop.

The familiar sound reached her eager ears and she turned back, relief flooding through her as she slipped the conch back into her pocket. Lord Yama and his bull appeared before her. He had come — he had heard her call. Yama dismounted and beckoned to Tara to step into the shadows.

"What is it, Tara? You look very troubled."

Tara folded her hands and bowed. To have the God of Death be so kind to her was unimaginable.

"Our village is in grave danger from Zarku and his army. We need your help, Lord Yama," she said in a shaky voice.

"Tara, I know all about Zarku and his cheap tricks. He has been capturing the souls of the villagers of Morni, Ropar, and hundreds of other villages. He has currently earned the goodwill of Kubera. But not for long ... not for long," said Lord Yama.

His face was a grim mask. He balled his right hand into a fist and smacked it into his left palm with a resounding thwack.

"Lord Yama, can you help us? We are going to the village tonight. My grandfather, Prabala, is going to face Zarku and force him to free the villagers. I am afraid that his skills may not be a match for Zarku. If you were to fight with us ..."

Lord Yama shook his head sadly. Tara's heart sank.

"Why not?" she asked.

"My hands are tied, Tara. I cannot do too much. I can only claim the souls of the dead. What Zarku is doing is evil. I cannot do the same or I will be banished forever from the clan of the gods. He is evil and will always be an outcast."

Tara's face fell. They would never have a chance.

"Have faith in your grandfather. He is more powerful than you think. He can and will defeat Zarku."

Tara shook her head. "Ananth and I have faced Zarku's army. They are so many and we are so few. I am very afraid."

Her chest heaved with sobs. She sank down on the ground and buried her head in her hands. Lord Yama clasped her thin, shaking shoulder.

"Tara, you worry too much. Everything will be all right. You don't need me."

Tara wiped her eyes with the back of her hand and stood up.

"But we do, Lord Yama, ... *we do*! You gave me the conch shell when I came back from the cave. You said you'd help me if I needed you."

Lord Yama watched her closely without uttering a word.

Tara knelt and clasped her hands together. "Lord Yama, you are most powerful and wise. A mere girl like me could never dream of helping you, but someday, *someday*, you might need my help. I will do anything you ask of me."

Yama threw back his head and laughed.

"Oh, Tara! You never fail to astound me with your bravery and, yes, sometimes your utter foolishness. But once again you have won me over. I will help you and will remember your words if I should need help *someday*."

"You promise?" she asked, looking into his coal-black eyes.

Lord Yama nodded. "Now, go back before you are missed. Tell no one about this," he warned.

Tara skipped back to the cave, smiling.

"What are you so happy about?" asked Ananth.

"Nothing, nothing at all," said Tara, though her eyes continued to sparkle.

"It's time to go," announced Prabala.

Everyone stopped what they were doing and stared at

him. He stood up straight and, in spite of the gaunt frame, the power and confidence that radiated from him stilled the doubts in their hearts.

"You will *all* do as I say. Our lives depend on this. No one will do as they please. No arguments. Is that understood?"

Everyone nodded.

Tara shouldered the heavy bundle she was used to carrying.

"Leave that, Tara," commanded Prabala. "We can fetch it later. Right now we need to get back to Morni as quickly as we can."

Tara dropped the bundle and followed Prabala out of the cave.

• • •

They began the descent to Morni. The path was steep and twisted, like the coils of a gigantic serpent. Tara was excited and nervous at the same time so that her stomach churned and her hands were icy. She strained her ears to catch the clip-clop of hooves. She did not hear anything.

I hope he does not desert us, she prayed.

Soma flooded the path with a silvery light. A biting wind swept down the mountainside. They descended the mountain in a single file. It became colder, and Tara's hands and feet grew more numb. The hairs in her nose were frozen from inhaling the frigid air. At every step a voice nagged her ...

You've forgotten something, Tara. Something very important.

Tara wracked her brains, but she couldn't think of anything. She patted the conch shell in her pocket. It was the most important thing she would need right now.

After what seemed like hours, a light twinkled in the distance: Morni!

They reached the outskirts of the village and the feeling of danger and panic was palpable. Tara's heart started hammering. She looked at Ananth. His smile looked more like a grimace. Suraj clutched Parvati's hand tightly. Gayatri followed silently, darting anxious looks around her at every step. Only Prabala strode forward confidently.

Not a sound disturbed the still air, which was heavy with the stench of fear. Prabala led the way to the nearest hut. He beckoned to Ananth and pointed to the hut. Ananth nodded and walked toward it. Prabala turned to the rest of the group, put a finger on his lips, and held up his palm. Then he turned and followed Ananth. All eyes turned to Ananth, who had peeped into the hut through the window and was now looking back, his eyes wide open with horror. Prabala quickened his pace. Tara could stand it no longer. She took a step in the direction of the hut and stopped.

"Ow," she yelped softly.

Parvati had reached out and grabbed Tara's plait to stop her from walking away.

"Stay here," hissed Parvati.

"I have to go, Mother," Tara replied in a very low murmur. "I must see what's going on." She slipped out of her mother's grasp before Parvati could utter another word and ran to take a look. Prabala and Ananth were already inside. Tara reached the window and peeped in. She clapped her hands to her mouth.

Inside were a mother and her two children, motionless. The woman's mouth was wide open in a silent scream. The first child was huddled close to his mother, crying. Tears, glistening like pearls in the silvery moonlight, were frozen on his cheeks. The second boy was sprawled near the door. He must have charged at whoever entered the hut and been flung aside. He lay on the ground, clutching his bleeding head.

The terror on their faces was so contagious that Tara shuddered. Could it have been Zarku who had entered? Unable to look upon them any longer, Tara turned and, on shaky legs, made her way back to her mother. Parvati shot her an angry look, but before she could say anything, Prabala and Ananth returned.

"It's horrible in there. Let's go. There is nothing we can do at the moment," said Prabala.

They made their way to the next hut and the next. Every hut was the same. The women and children were frozen in eternal terror.

"Do you notice a pattern, Dada?" Ananth asked Prabala in a whisper.

"The men are all gone," said Prabala in a grim voice.

"Zarku has claimed all the men of the village."

"This means that we will be fighting our own friends and family," Tara whispered in dismay.

"They are now under the influence of Zarku," said Prabala. "Till they are freed, they are all Vetalas. If you don't kill them first, they will kill you. We've seen enough. Let's go to my hut."

They passed a few white-washed huts that glinted silver in the light of the full moon and reached Prabala's hut. It was deserted, yet they moved cautiously. Prabala pushed open the rickety door that hung awkwardly from a single hinge. It opened inward and moonlight lit up the interior. Parvati moaned.

"Oh Father, just look at the state of your beloved home."

Prabala looked around with a pained expression. He avoided stepping on the pieces of clay and glass that littered the floor. Blood and feathers lay strewn about. The stench of decaying meat, soured milk, and vomit was so strong that Gayatri rushed to the window and retched. She took a deep breath, trying to draw some fresh air into her lungs.

"This is ghastly," she gasped.

"He has defiled my home, the evil wretch," thundered Prabala. "He will pay for this."

"Dada, I can smell something burning," said Suraj.

Prabala looked down at Suraj, who was tugging at his dhoti.

"Are you sure, Suraj? I cannot smell any ... you're

right! Something is burning." He strode to the window and looked out. A faint glow was visible behind the huts. The smell of burning grew stronger and his nostrils flared. He went back to the centre of the hut.

"Someone find me a lantern. Quick."

Everyone scattered.

"Tara, come here," called out Prabala.

Tara came up to him. Prabala drew out the rudraksha from his dhoti, where it was tucked securely at the waist, and handed it to Tara.

"Tie this on my right arm, hurry," he said, shifting his weight from one foot to the other.

Tara tied it to his arm with trembling hands. Prabala continued to twist and turn, trying to peer out the window and to the back of the hut at the same time.

"I've found one," Ananth called out from the kitchen. "But it's broken and empty."

"Never mind, give it here," said Prabala.

He tapped the lantern with his staff and uttered a few words. A flame leapt up and he thrust the lantern back into Ananth's hands.

"I want all of you to stay in this hut. I am going to put a spell around it. You will be safe here. Zarku or the Vetalas will be unable to enter the hut."

"I cannot let you go alone, Father," said Parvati. "I am coming with you."

"So am I," said Ananth.

"No one is coming with me. I want no arguments.

213

This is not a game."

The smell of burning was a lot stronger. Light flickered outside the window and the glow was almost as bright as the lantern in Ananth's hands.

"Oh my God! He has set the village on fire," shrieked Gayatri. "All those women and children in the huts, they'll be burnt and they won't even know it."

Her voice cracked and she started sobbing.

"Not yet, Gayatri," said Prabala. "The houses are not on fire. Zarku has lit a ring of fire around the village to prevent anyone from escaping, including us. The fire will creep inward slowly, but before that I will stop him. I MUST."

"But you will need help," Tara piped in. "Let me come with you."

"No, I will go alone. This amulet is all the protection I need. I will concentrate better if I know all of you are safe. Stay here till I return."

"But," started Tara.

"Enough," roared Prabala. He flung his hand at the window. "Just look outside. Do you think I can fight that madman if even one member of my family is in danger? Not a word more ... from ANYONE!" he shouted as he pounded his staff on the floor. The amulet slid off his arm and fell to the ground, landing under a piece of broken clay. No one saw it but Tara. They were too busy staring at Prabala's thunderous face.

Tara went cold; she had not tied the rudraksha tightly

enough. She had to tell him and re-tie it.

"Grandfather ...," said Tara hesitantly.

"NOT ANOTHER WORD, I SAID!" he bellowed.

"But all I wanted to say was ..."

Prabala's face twisted with rage and his nostrils flared as he breathed heavily.

"Enough, Tara! You should know when to keep your mouth shut," said Parvati.

Suraj, Ananth, and Gayatri observed the heated exchange between Prabala and Tara in silence. Prabala strode to the door, turned, and looked back at Parvati.

"Your daughter has become too disobedient. Teach her some respect."

"I'll talk to her," said Parvati, shielding Tara with her body, pushing her to the back of the room. "I am sorry, Father."

Prabala whirled on his heel and sprinted out the door. Tara turned to Parvati.

"Mother, listen to me: Dada's amulet has fallen off; he does not have the power and protection he thinks he has."

Everyone looked aghast as Tara lunged forward and picked up the amulet from under the piece of clay. Ananth ran to the window.

"He's just about to put a spell on the hut," yelled Ananth. "Let me go with him, I'm stronger."

Tara looked at Parvati as she held up the amulet. Parvati nodded as tears filled her eyes. Tara shot a triumphant look at Ananth. His expression was sulky.

"Go quickly, child. May Lord Ganesh protect you," said Parvati.

Tara shot through the kitchen and jumped out the back door just as Prabala's voice, chanting the spell, died away and a shimmery outline formed around the hut. But Tara did not wait a second longer. She raced round the hut and sprinted after Prabala, who had already disappeared into the shadows of the night.

CHAPTER 16
THE BATTLE OF THE HEALERS

The stench of burning grew stronger as Prabala raced to the centre of the village. The flames surrounding the village were now clearly visible as they leapt up to the black sky. Acrid clouds of black smoke billowed up, creating a haze. He stopped short of the clearing and darted behind a tree to survey the scene.

The banyan tree in the centre of the village was ablaze. He clenched his hand into a fist and shook it in helpless rage.

Tara, racing to catch up with Prabala, also saw the tree. She was appalled at losing a part of her childhood — a landmark that had always been there. To see it go up in flames felt like a part of her body was on fire. But what were those moving shadows under the tree? Her heart hammered loudly and blood roared through her ears. Those shadows were the Vetalas, scores and scores of them, gathered round the tree watching — *enjoying* it going up in flames. They leapt and capered around it in an uncoordinated way, as if jerked by an unseen puppeteer.

Keeping to the shadows, Prabala inched around the clearing one stealthy step at a time. No one seemed to have noticed him. The green-black shadows continued their weird dancing around the banyan tree. The singing, which sounded more like wailing, sent a chill up Tara's spine. It sounded like someone being strangled, very slowly and very painfully. She called out to Prabala but he did not hear her above the commotion.

Suddenly, Prabala sprawled on the ground. He fell face down and did not move. What had happened? She could not see anything. What was going on? She forced herself to stand still, digging her nails into the tree trunk to keep from running to help her grandfather. Mad laughter filled the air. Shadows materialized next to Prabala and he was dragged toward the banyan tree. Closer to the fire, Tara could see that he was surrounded by the Vetalas. The crowd parted and Zarku strode forward. Tara turned icy cold and her mouth was dry. She turned and retched into the bushes. In her mind, she could still hear the agonized screams of the two men that Zarku had burned alive in front of her in the mountains.

Get a grip, Tara, the small voice inside her said, and the nauseous feeling slowly abated. But while her stomach had stopped heaving, her heart continued to hammer.

You wanted to help your grandfather, you wanted to be brave. Well, here you are. What are you going to do about it?

Shut up! she told the voice.

Coward! Run back to Mummy, said the little voice.

Shut up, I'm trying to think, she snapped back.

The little fight within herself made her feel braver and more in control.

I have to do something. But what?

She peered anxiously from behind the tree. Prabala was hidden by a sea of green bodies. The smell of rotten flesh reached her and she wrinkled her nose, trying to control the heaving in her stomach.

Yes, help your grandfather by vomiting all over the Vetalas, the sarcastic voice piped in. *That will surely drive them away.*

Gradually, her ebbing courage returned. With it returned that nagging feeling that she'd forgotten something very important. *Not now,* she told herself as she crept forward to get a better look. Zarku had raised his hands and all sound and movement stopped. The Vetalas gazed at him in anticipation.

"My brave men, today is a triumph for us. We have the great Prabala in our power and the rest of his family is back in the village. Let us rid ourselves of his evil influence forever. His soul will please Kubera!"

His voice was growing steadily louder and he shrieked the last few words. The crowd was roused and they were all yelling and clapping in response.

Tara strained to get a glimpse of her grandfather. She crouched low to the ground and at last, between the milling green feet, she saw him. He was unconscious and tied to a stake very close to the burning tree.

How could this happen to her grandfather? Did he have no power at all without the rudraksha? He was faking it, for sure. He would wake up in a moment and strike them all dead, starting with Zarku. Tara waited and watched as the flames came closer and closer to Prabala's inert body.

"Wake up, Dada, *wake up*," she muttered under her breath.

Zarku's speech had roused the Vetalas so much that they were almost out of control. They leapt, gibbered, and danced like animals around Prabala's prone body. Zarku surveyed the scene of madness and smiled deeply, caressing his bald head lovingly.

"Please wake up, Dada, they are going to kill you," pleaded Tara softly, hoping her earnest prayers would reach him.

He did not move.

She looked at the rudraksha clasped in her hand and knew what she had to do. Her knees shook and her armpits were damp with sweat.

She knelt and prayed. *Lord Soma, Lord Yama, help me, please.* She looked up at the sky and noticed thick clouds on the horizon. They seemed to be sailing toward her at an incredible speed. As soon as they reached the banyan tree a deluge of water rained down and doused the flames. Zarku looked up angrily, unable to believe it.

Just then, the moon went out. The village centre was

plunged into darkness. Tara had memorized the exact spot where Prabala had been tied. As soon as the light went out, she ran like an arrow released from a bow, straight to the spot where Prabala was tied.

There was utter pandemonium with people bumping into each other. All of a sudden, the yells became louder and more agonized.

"Thwack!"

"Thump!"

"Aarrg!"

"Ooooooff!"

The air was thick with guttural grunts.

Above it all, Zarku shrieked, "Get me some light, you morons! *Get me some light!*"

Tara bumped into cold flesh and the smell of decay enveloped her. She pinched her nose tightly so that she would not faint, and kept going. Finally, she touched warm flesh. Dada! Feeling her way to the back of the stake, she started untying the rope that bound his hands, all the while whispering in his ear, "Wake up, Dada. Please wake up."

There was no response, and she was getting desperate. She bit his shoulder. Prabala woke up with a cry.

"Ow!"

"Shhhh, Grandfather, it's me, Tara."

"Tara, what you are doing here? What happened? Why is it so dark?"

"I could not let you face Zarku alone, Dada. I slipped out of the hut before you put the spell on it."

"Tara, that was a very dangerous and silly thing to do," said Prabala, sternly. "Now both our lives are in danger. How will I face your mother if anything happens to you?"

"Your amulet fell off in the hut when you yelled at me. You need this and I had to bring it to you," she whispered, scrabbling at the knots that bound Prabala's hands and feet.

"Tara, you are truly my star. I am sorry I yelled at you," said Prabala. "Hurry! Untie my hands and then give me the rudraksha."

"Thwack!"

"Thump!"

The sounds and the yells continued. Tara finally managed to untie the ropes. Her nails were torn and bleeding, but she ignored the pain.

"We have very little time, Dada," she whispered urgently. "Can you walk? We need to get away from here. I'll tie the amulet on your arm and then you can take over."

"I can. Let's go."

The next moment, the clearing was bathed in light. Zarku had lit another fire, which remained untouched by the steady rain. It burned a bright red and illuminated the clearing for miles.

Lord Yama waded through the Vetalas, giving them a taste of his mace.

Both Soma and Lord Yama had come to their rescue. But it had not been enough. They had still not gotten away in time. She had not even been able to tie the amulet on her grandfather's arm. They were lost. Terror and panic spiralled through her body. The horizon seemed to be tilting.

Zarku advanced toward Tara, his third eye bulging dangerously in his forehead.

"So *this* is the busybody that has ruined my plans," he said in a calm voice, all the while stroking his bald head. "*Wonderful.* One more to kill tonight, and it will be my pleasure to start with you, Tara."

"NO!" roared Prabala. "You have a grudge against me. Kill me and spare the child."

"This is no child. She's a demon. I should have killed her ages ago," snarled Zarku.

Prabala hobbled to his feet and stood in front of Tara.

"You will have to kill me first."

"Get away, you pathetic old fool," said Zarku, and with a swipe of his hand he pushed Prabala aside.

Prabala fell to the ground and did not move.

"Dada!" wailed Tara, lunging forward.

Zarku slapped her hard. She went sprawling to the ground and hit her head against a rock. Her ears rang and warm liquid trickled into her left eye. Her head throbbed savagely.

"*You meddlesome witch*! This is the last time you poke your nose where it does not belong."

Red and yellow sparks flew out of Zarku's third eye. Tara was mesmerized. Blood dribbled out of the corner of his mouth. His black eyes glowed and his bald head reflected the red light. He reached out his talon-like hand and grasped her wrist.

"LET ME GO," she screamed. "Dada, help me! HELLLLPPPP!"

Prabala remained unconscious.

She looked up at Zarku's face through a mist of tears. His third eye was opening. Suddenly, she remembered the silver anklet! It had saved her the last time she had encountered Zarku. It was in her bundle of clothes, back in the cave ... she was doomed. But she wasn't going to give up without a fight.

Tara squirmed and thrashed wildly, trying to free herself. Something hard smacked into her lip and the salty taste of blood seeped into her mouth. The mirror that she always wore around her neck had fallen out of her kurta. It flashed red, reflecting the fire, as she wrestled to get free of Zarku's grasp.

Zarku's eye was halfway open and heat poured out of it like molten lava. Tara's skin was starting to blister and the pain was unbearable. With her free hand, she grabbed the mirror and turned it toward the red beam just as his eye opened completely. The full force of that lethal gaze ricocheted back to Zarku. He screamed with agony as his skin seared and melted.

"AAAAAIIIIIIEEEEEEEE!" he howled.

The mirror heated up instantly and scorched Tara's hand, but she held the mirror steady, and within seconds

Zarku was a mound of black ash.

Tears of relief and exhaustion poured down Tara's cheeks as she crawled to her grandfather, who was still lying unconscious.

"Finally, I can give this back to you, Dada," she said in a frail voice.

She unclenched the hand that Zarku had held in his relentless grip. The skin on her wrist was red and raw, but she had not let go of the precious amulet. Aware of its immense value to her grandfather, she had held it so tightly that the corrugated surface of the rudraksha seed had imprinted itself in the soft skin of her palm. Her hand, and the seed, were covered with blood. Shaking with exhaustion, she tied the seed onto her grandfather's arm. He stirred almost immediately as the amulet and all its powers infused his body.

Tara's vision blurred. She saw Prabala's eyes open. She smiled to herself: he was safe, Zarku was dead. And then she lay down on the ground in complete exhaustion.

Prabala sprang to his feet and surveyed the scene. The Vetalas stood in silence now that their leader was dead. Lord Yama stood to one side, his mace on his shoulder. The red fire burnt on. Prabala moved Tara out of harm's way. He kneeled in the clearing and prayed to the Rain God. The rain that had doused the banyan tree earlier continued to fall steadily, but it was now accompanied by lightning. Huge black clouds hung low in the sky and the lightning grew stronger as Prabala's chanting grew louder.

Suddenly, a deafening clap of thunder and an enormous bolt of lightning shot out of the sky.

The Vetalas, who had been standing dazed, were woken from their stupors. Then, they changed. Their skin gradually lost the green hue, their feet turned the right way around, and they recognized each other. Scores and scores of men hugged each other, free of the hypnotic influence of Zarku. Their salty tears mingled with the icy rain and washed away the filth of their bodies and souls.

Prabala approached Lord Yama and, pressing his hands together, bowed to the God of Death.

"Lord Yama, I thank you for your help today."

Lord Yama inclined his head.

"Your granddaughter is the one who convinced me. She is a brave young girl."

"Yes, she is," said Prabala, looking back at Tara with pride.

"I have one last request for you, my Lord."

"Speak."

"Can you please take the ashes of Zarku and bury them in a deep, dark place so that he will never defile this earth again?"

"I will not touch the ashes of a soul so corrupt. I will send one of my messengers to collect and dispose of them. Leave them in a tightly sealed earthen pot by the banyan tree."

Prabala nodded. "It will be done, my Lord. Thank you once again."

Lord Yama got onto his bull and disappeared into the forest.

Prabala picked up Tara. The girl was barely conscious, but she still managed a faint smile. He kissed her forehead gently and strode back to his hut. Tendrils of pink and gold adorned the sky like banners heralding the approach of a joyous day.

CHAPTER 17
THE END AND THE BEGINNING

When Tara awoke she was back in Prabala's hut, her head cradled in her mother's lap. Parvati peered at her anxiously.

"Tara, are you all right?"

"I'm fine, Mother. How is Grandfather?"

"He is well. He has gone with Ananth to remove all traces of Zarku from the village and to talk to the Panchayat."

"I must go and help him."

"Haven't you done enough, Tara? You have changed so much from the time I left you. I am very happy and extremely proud."

Tara smiled.

"Yes, these last few weeks have made me grow up in a hurry. And you know the best thing?" said Tara, her eyes sparkling. "I'm not so scared all the time."

Parvati hugged Tara. Suraj, not wanting to be left out, joined in the hug.

"I wish Father were here," said Tara. "It would be like old times, before you went away."

"I want to see your father, too," said Parvati. "We have to wait till Prabala gets back. And ... here he is."

Prabala walked in with Ananth.

"Looks like our little tigress is awake," he said, smiling at Tara.

"Don't say that, Dada. Has everything returned to normal in Morni?"

"Yes. The men who were Vetalas have all returned to their normal selves. As soon as Zarku died, the spell weakened. They've all gone to their families now."

"And the women and my friends?" asked Tara.

"Can you not hear them?"

And Tara realized that there indeed was a lot of noise in the background. The village sounded normal once more.

"Father, where is Shiv?"

"Ah yes, Parvati. Shiv is at home waiting for you."

"And Kali?"

"The villagers realized that it was she and her father Dushta who had invited Zarku to the village. They are holding Kali and Layla prisoner in one of the huts."

"I want to talk to Kali, and ask her what drove her to do this," said Parvati, distressed.

"Go to Shiv, first."

They all went together: Parvati, Tara, and Suraj.

The street thronged with villagers, all discussing the catastrophe.

Normal. Things are back to normal, thought Tara, breathing in the cold, clean air. A big grin was plastered on her face and her heart was light as they raced home. As they neared the hut, they slowed down. There was no sound from inside. Parvati stepped in. Tara and Suraj followed. Shiv sat in a corner, his head in his hands.

"Shiv!" said Parvati.

"Father!" Tara and Suraj yelled out in unison.

Shiv looked up in amazement. He jumped to his feet and ran to them.

"You are back. I thought I had lost my family forever."

He embraced them all at once.

"Prabala told me everything," said Shiv. "Why did you go away, Parvati? We could have convinced the villagers together."

"I had to go away, Shiv, or the children would have suffered. The villagers are so ignorant. Sooner or later we would all have been in danger."

"Kali is to blame for the hell we have been through these last few months," Shiv said, his face twisted in pain and disgust.

"Yes, Shiv, she is to blame for everything that we and Morni have been through. I thought she was my friend and I tried my best to be a good friend to her, but she was too jealous of our happiness."

Parvati clutched Shiv's hand as she wiped her tears away.

"All I remember is going to her hut one evening. There I met Zarku, and after that I do not remember anything."

"You mean you do not remember that Kali ill-treated us and starved us?" asked Tara, her eyes wide with surprise.

He shook his head.

"I am so sorry, my dearest hearts. It must have been terrible to think that your father did not care about you at all."

"Zarku must have hypnotized you so that you would not remember your true family or love your children," said Parvati. "I think Kali was counting on Zarku killing Prabala and me so that she would have you to herself forever."

Shiv wept silently.

"We understand, Father," said Tara, hugging him. "You don't need to say any more."

"We are together now," said Parvati, in a whisper. "That is all that matters."

"And what is to become of Kali?" asked Tara.

"She will be lynched tomorrow," replied Shiv.

"No, that would be very wrong," said Parvati. "Taking a life is only in the hands of the gods. We have to stop it."

"She deserves to die a painful death," said Shiv, his face a grim mask. "She has brought so much unhappiness into our lives. She deserves it."

"No one deserves death," said Parvati. "We should turn her out of the village. That will be punishment enough."

"Mother, what about Layla?" asked Suraj. "Will she go with Kali?"

"No," said Parvati. "We will keep her. It is not the child's fault that the mother is so evil."

"You are wrong, Mother," said Tara with passion in her voice. "Layla is growing up to be exactly like her mother. She is evil! She used to enjoy getting Suraj and me into trouble. She will be just like Kali when she grows up, believe me, Mother."

"Tara is right," said Suraj, very forcefully.

"That's enough, children. The elders will decide the fate of Kali and Layla. You both need to sleep for a bit. You have been awake all night."

Parvati helped Shiv to roll out the bedding and in a short while the children were asleep. Shiv and Parvati continued talking late into the day.

●●●

That evening, after all the families had rested, the elders met in the village centre. The entire village turned up. Tara and Suraj went on ahead and settled themselves near the Panchayat.

"Look at our tree; it's gone," said Raka in a grief-stricken voice.

Villagers bemoaned the loss of their beloved tree, which had provided shade for countless years. A burnt stump, sticking out of the ground like an eyesore, was all that was left.

"Gather round, people of Morni," said Raka. "We need to make some serious decisions."

They all sat solemnly, facing Raka. Prabala came striding up and joined them. A few minutes later, Parvati and Shiv arrived. The meeting started.

"Bring Kali here," Raka commanded.

A dishevelled Kali was led to the meeting from a nearby hut, where she had been held captive. She kicked and screamed profanities at the villagers as they dragged her in front of the Panchayat.

As Kali passed Tara sitting in the crowd, she freed herself and lunged at Tara's throat.

Tara slapped Kali's hand away and gave her a hard push. It had been an instinctive reaction. And it felt really good.

Villagers restrained Kali none too gently and dumped her unceremoniously on the ground. A sea of accusing eyes bored into her. The people were barely able to stop themselves from stoning her to death.

Raka started speaking.

"We have had a terrible fate befall our village since Zarku arrived. We all know now that it was Kali and her father Dushta that invited them here. It is lucky for Dushta that he was killed in last night's fight or he too would be standing trial with you. Why, Kali? Why did you bring this evil to our village?" asked Raka.

Kali glared at the Panchayat wordlessly, with blood-shot eyes. Her hair was unkempt and surrounded her head like a black halo. Remnants of the red juice from a betel nut dribbled out at the side of her mouth. No one could look upon her for very long without a shudder of revulsion.

"Speak, Kali, or you will be tried without a defence," said Raka in a stern voice.

Kali spat in his direction and looked away.

Raka rose to his feet, his eyes flashing with anger.

"You will be stoned at dawn. A person like you is too terrible to let loose upon the world."

Parvati stood up, graceful and beautiful — the complete opposite of Kali. All faces turned to her like sunflowers to the sun.

"Can we not spare her life, Rakaji?" she asked humbly, folding her hands. "Do we have the right to take her life — or any life, for that matter? We are not gods, but mere mortals."

"Parvati, you and your children have suffered the most at her hands. She and Zarku almost killed your children. How can you even think of sparing her life? No, I will not hear of it."

Prabala rose.

"Raka, I think we should consider turning her out of the village. How different will we be from Zarku if we have Kali's blood on our hands? Do we want to be called murderers?"

A lot of noise and debate ensued as the villagers shouted their opinions. The Panchayat whispered among themselves, debating the best course of action. Kali glared at Parvati and Prabala.

"Quiet, everyone," said Raka, holding up his staff.

The villagers fell silent and looked at him expectantly.

"The Panchayat has decided. Kali, you will leave the village immediately. You are to take nothing. Do not come back. There will be guards around the village. If you ever show your face here again, you will be killed immediately. Do you understand?"

"What about my daughter?" asked Kali.

"I will look after her," said Parvati.

"NO! I will take her with me," said Kali, her voice harsh and cold. "I'd rather choke the life out of her with my own hands than let you bring her up," she spat out at Parvati.

"You will leave alone," said Raka. "No child should ever be exposed to your evil presence, not even your own child. I pray to Lord Ganesh that none of your tainted blood runs through her veins."

Kali spat and shrieked every curse she ever knew as the villagers dragged her to the edge of the village and threw her on the road.

"Go away and never again darken our village with your unholy presence," said Raka with a tone of absolute finality.

Kali got up and stumbled away in the darkness.

The villagers looked at each other with weariness and relief. Raka kneeled before Prabala and touched his feet.

"We will never doubt you again, Prabala. You have

saved us all from a fate worse than death. As Zarku's army," and he shuddered as he said the name, "the villagers would have roamed the earth killing and plundering forever, without hope of life or peace of death."

He touched his forehead to Prabala's feet. All the villagers supplicated themselves in front of him, murmuring their thanks. Parvati smiled at Prabala, tears sparkling in her eyes. It was good to be home again.

● ● ●

Kali stumbled in the darkness, trying to find her way to another village. It was darker than the darkness in her heart. Even Soma had withdrawn from her evil presence that night. She cursed every member of the Panchayat aloud each time she stumbled or stubbed her toe against a rock.

Sound was her only guide now. She heard the gurgling of a river. Tired and thirsty, she crawled toward it. The dry foliage turned damp as she got closer, and seeped through her clothes. She saw a faint, reddish glow through the trees. Perplexed, she crept forward to investigate. It grew stronger as she neared the edge of the river. She stood up and approached it cautiously. Entangled in the roots of a large gulmohur tree was an earthen pot. Though it was sealed, blood-red light seeped from the edges. Kali stood some distance away, staring at it, afraid to go any closer.

"Come here, you stupid woman," said a cold and extremely familiar voice. "It's me."

ACKNOWLEDGEMENTS

There are several people I'd like to thank for bringing this book to publication. My sincere thanks to:

Marsha Skrypuch, for her overwhelming generosity and gentle nudge in the right direction.

The Private Kidcrit critique group, which helped me hone the manuscript to its current sleek state. I'd especially like to thank Marsha Skrypuch, Helaine Becker, Hélène Boudreau, Marina Cohen, Elizabeth B., Martha Martin, Carmen Wright, Natalie Hyde, and Nancy Runstedler for their excellent critiques.

Valerie Sherrard for her timely support and advice.

Anne, Peter, and Michael Lilly for their enthusiasm and feedback during the early stages of this manuscript.

The Bedford Book Club boys: Aftab, Danny, Duncan, Jon, Peter, and Sam, who provided great insight into what makes a book "awesome."

Rahul, for his infinite patience while this manuscript took shape over four years and twenty rewrites.

Aftab, who was my first reader and loyal fan.

Zenia and Rayhan, for their animated support.

My wonderful and warm editor Barry Jowett, whose infectious humour and enthusiasm made working to deadlines bearable, especially the weekend that HP7 was released.

And finally the fabulous team at Dundurn: Kirk Howard, Beth Bruder, Jennifer Scott, Alison Carr, Ali Pennels, and Margaret Bryant for all their hard work in bringing this book to life and for believing in me.